WAKE THE DEAD

WAKE THE DEAD

Dead For Good Book Four

STACY CLAFLIN

NOLON KING

STERLING & STONE

Chapter One

CHINK, chink, clink.

Brad rolled over and groaned, trying to figure out what the noise was.

Metal on metal.

He sat up, rubbing at the awful kink in his neck as he looked around the concrete walls of his cell. Memories of the night before flooded back like a nightmare.

Except this was real life. He was in a holding cell in Pine Harbor's local police station. He'd been accused of a murder he didn't commit.

He'd committed plenty of murders. They were all legitimate killings of horrible people who had escaped the law, sanctioned by the government and carried out by assassins like Brad. He'd never been caught — or even suspected — for any of those.

Just for the murders he didn't commit.

And this was number three, but the first to get him arrested.

Where was his lawyer? As the cops had dragged him away in front of his family and neighbors, he'd told Faye

1

where to find the number. He should've been bailed out by now.

He wasn't sure what time it was, but given that it felt like he'd slept for hours, it had to be morning.

Had his wife been unable to find the envelope? Was the attorney out of town or otherwise unreachable? Even if that were the case, one of her associates should have jumped in to help.

None of this made any sense.

He didn't even know who he was being accused of killing. All the detective had told him was they'd found some bloody knife with his fingerprints.

Kurt had framed him.

He still had his one phone call. The previous night, he'd refused. Wanted to save that for an emergency.

It was getting close.

Brad rose from the bed — if it could even be called that, a sorry excuse of a mattress lying directly on top of the concrete floor. He twisted his neck back and forth, then stretched out his arms and legs. There were several knots up and down his spine.

He ignored them and pounded on the door. If anyone was nearby, they would hear him. And he wouldn't stop until they came over and spoke with him.

Until he got answers.

It took a few minutes, but a young uniformed officer appeared on the other side of the window looking mildly annoyed. "Can I help you?"

"Where is my attorney?"

"No idea."

"She hasn't been here? Called? Anything?"

The officer sighed. "Not that I'm aware. Are you ready for breakfast?"

"The only thing I want is my lawyer."

"Can't help you with that." She started to walk away.

"Wait!"

She turned back around. "Yes?"

"Has my wife called?"

"I don't know. What's her name?"

"Faye Morris."

"I'll check." She spun around.

"She was supposed to call my attorney!"

"Like I said, I'll check." The officer hurried away.

Brad hit the wall, ignoring the pain in his knuckles.

What now? If he had his cell phone, he could make any number of calls. Could call for another lawyer. Though he'd prefer the one in that envelope that he'd tucked away for an occasion like this, at this point, he'd take just about anyone who was at least a step above public defender.

Would it come down to needing to lower his standards? Take a PD lawyer? If it meant getting out from the holding cell, he might have to go down that road.

Then he could go home and demand attention from the attorney he needed. Getting out of this rat hole was only the beginning. He would still have the charge hanging over him. And he didn't know what kind of battle it would be to get those dropped.

It wouldn't be easy this time. Before, he'd been framed by his neighbors. Twice. And he'd managed to clear his name without so much as an arrest.

But Kurt knew what he was doing. He wouldn't make the kinds of mistakes that an amateur would.

But Brad didn't even know who he'd supposedly killed.

Kurt could've even known a dirty cop. The department had seized all of his knives after Duke's murder. Or had it been Allison's? Either way, Brad hadn't gotten them back yet, thanks to red tape.

His name had been cleared, so he'd thought he was good.

So much for that.

He'd have to make sure his lawyer checked the inventory of every knife seized, in case the murder weapon had been stolen from an evidence locker. He hoped that was the case — that would make it easy to show he'd been framed.

The officer walked by the window again.

Brad leaped over, ignoring his aches and pains. "Did you reach my lawyer? Or my wife?"

She shook her head no.

"Would you at least tell me who I'm being accused of killing? Last night you said I had to wait for legal representation, but I don't know how long that will be. At least tell me what's going on."

Her expression soured. "Would you like to use your phone call?"

Should he? If he couldn't reach Faye, that would blow his one shot. And he might very well need to call a lawyer from the yellow pages, if she didn't get his lawyer on the case soon.

"Not yet."

"Then I can't help you."

"This has to be illegal." He slapped the window. "If you're going to arrest me, at least tell me who I supposedly killed."

"*I* didn't arrest you. Are you ready for breakfast yet?"

He glowered before turning his back to her.

This couldn't be happening. It had to be a bad dream that he couldn't wake from.

Except it wasn't.

Brad paced again, muttering to himself.

During two out of three of his last hits, he'd been

attacked. Not that it had stopped him from taking out his targets.

Brad had managed to ward off his attackers and still get his jobs done.

The only reason he didn't run into opposition for the last one was because he kept his boss in the dark. Didn't tell Kurt that he was going out for the kill.

There was only one explanation for that.

Kurt had tried to kill him twice, and when that didn't work, this was a new trick. Planting evidence and getting Brad arrested.

Kurt seemed to prefer having his people in jail rather than dead. Unlike his dad. Ralf just killed his assassins.

That was the threat that always hung over their heads. It kept them all in line.

Nobody wanted to trigger the next Felix incident.

Brad cracked his knuckles.

It was time to use his phone call.

Chapter Two

FAYE PLACED two more toaster pastries in the toaster and rubbed her temples. It had been the longest night — and that was saying something after the year they'd had. But watching Brad get cuffed and loaded into the cop car had taken the cake. She'd thought the accusations from neighbors and police were bad before. This was an actual arrest, a neighborhood spectacle.

Hadley entered the kitchen. "I seriously can't believe you're making us go to school today."

"Dad's going to get out of jail, honey. We need to carry on with our lives."

Her daughter scowled. Her pregnant daughter who had been seeing the man next door before he'd been murdered — by one of the assassins Brad worked with, who'd made it look like Brad's work.

This was definitely the worst year of Faye's life. She didn't know how it could get any worse. A dangerous thought, but here she was.

Hadley grabbed milk from the fridge. "Nobody else has asked about Nate, have they?"

Faye closed her eyes and drew in a deep breath. Then there was *that* mess. One of Hadley's schoolmates had been threatening her, and in self-defense, she'd accidentally killed him.

Now they were covering up that crime.

Worst year ever.

"Mom?"

"No, nobody's asked about him that I know of."

Zeke came into the kitchen and snagged a pastry from the toaster just after it popped up. "Hot, hot!" He tossed it on a plate, blowing on his fingers.

Hadley rolled her eyes at him.

Zeke turned to Faye. "We really have to go to school today?"

"I already tried to talk her out of it." Hadley sighed dramatically. "She's not budging."

"But Dad's in jail!"

"I *know*."

Faye handed him a glass of orange juice. "And he'll be out soon. You kids are going to school, and I'm going into the salon."

"What about Grandma?" Zeke gulped down his drink.

"She'll have to come in with me."

"That sounds like fun."

"We're all doing what we have to until your dad gets back."

"The lawyer said she'd get him out?"

Faye sighed. "I haven't spoken to an attorney yet."

The kids both gave her incredulous expressions.

"I couldn't reach the one Dad wanted me to call. She never answered, so I called Kurt. He has access to all kinds of attorneys, and he always takes care of his people."

"His assassins, you mean," Zeke corrected.

"Not so loud!" Faye glared at him. "Grandma or little Luna could come in at any moment."

"Like it matters now."

"It *does*."

Hadley crossed her arms. "So, Kurt promised that his lawyer would get Dad out?"

Faye nodded. "He promised he'd put his best guy on it."

"But what if they have a knife that Dad really used to kill someone?"

"Your father said it was planted, so I believe him. He says he always gets rid of evidence."

"What if he messed up one time?" Hadley asked. "That's all it takes, you know."

Faye held her gaze for a moment. "He knows what he's doing. Your freedom depends on it."

Hadley's mouth formed a straight line.

"Burn!" Zeke snorted.

She shoved him. "Don't you have an eighties movie to watch?"

"Stop," Faye warned. "I thought you two were getting along now."

Zeke shot his sister a glare. "She didn't stop being annoying."

"Neither did you," Hadley snapped.

Faye counted to ten silently. "Get to school, you two. I need to make sure your sister and grandma are almost ready. I have to leave soon, and they still need breakfast."

Hadley grabbed an apple before hurrying from the room.

Zeke refilled the toaster with pastries and turned to his phone.

Faye leaned against the counter and pinched the bridge

of her nose. She'd been up much of the night, worried about Brad in the police station. Was he forced to spend the night with real criminals? Had the lawyer spoken with him yet?

Kurt had told her not to worry about a thing. Easier said than done.

She hoped she hadn't made a mistake, turning to her husband's boss. Brad had expressed concerns about both the Bergmanns lately, but who else was she going to ask? If only the attorney Brad wanted wasn't unreachable.

And she had no idea how to pick the right one for something like this.

Maybe she should try calling the number again, now that it was morning. Just in case. It seemed unlikely, but Brad could be upset about having to deal with one of Kurt's attorneys instead of his own — especially if he didn't trust his boss.

But nobody else knew about the assassinations. If anyone could help Brad, it was Kurt. And despite Brad's reservations, Kurt had been really nice to them. Especially recently. Brad's boss had paid for Faye's home hair salon construction. And his guys had gotten the job done really fast. Sure, it was noisy for a while, and Brad had been on edge with so many people in the house, but now Faye had the opportunity to open her own business. Finally was able to give notice at work. That was something she'd wanted to do for a long time. Now it was just a matter of hanging on until her grand opening.

Less than two weeks.

The toaster popped up, startling her.

Zeke grabbed the rest of his breakfast.

She reminded him to hurry, then went to check on Luna and Dianne. They were watching cartoons together.

"You two need to grab cold cereal quickly, if you're going to have time to eat."

Luna jumped up with a smile. "You never let me eat cereal!"

"Not *never*. Hurry up." Faye tried to help Dianne up, but she insisted on doing it herself, despite her casts and stitches.

"I'll be okay here alone for a few hours. You don't need to babysit me."

"It isn't babysitting. I'm going to give you a haircut. Do you think you want the same style, or do you want to be bold and try something new?"

"Call it what you want, but it's still babysitting." She made her way to the kitchen.

Faye passed Zeke in the hall.

He wiped powdered sugar from his mouth. "Can you take me to the store tonight?"

"Seriously?" she exclaimed. "What's so important?"

His expression lit up. "I have the money I need to buy all the equipment to start my gaming channel! I just need to get the stuff, or at least a gift card to order it online."

Faye sighed. "You need to learn about timing."

"What do you mean?"

"Your dad's in jail, and you're talking to me about going to the store for a video game."

She'd never seen him look so insulted. "It's more than *just* a game — it's the biggest game! Everyone's playing it, and gamers with channels are making serious cash off it. Seriously."

She shooed him to the door. "Hurry up before you miss the bus."

"So, you'll think about it?" He pleaded with his eyes.

"Zeke, go. I can't promise anything right now." Faye

turned to see Luna pouring so much milk into her cereal that it was about to overflow. "Stop!"

She hurried over and grabbed the carton just in time to stop a mini disaster.

It was going to be a really long day.

Chapter Three

HADLEY PARKED her car and stared at the main school building, pressure building behind her eyes. If only it wouldn't look suspicious, she'd gladly switch to online school. Or even homeschooling, at this point. But people were still eyeing her about Nate's death — no, his disappearance. Nobody knew he was dead. That she'd killed him.

It'd been an accident, and it never would've happened if he hadn't been threatening her. If his dad hadn't threatened her first, she never would've been carrying that knife around.

Now everything was screwed up. Literally everything. She hadn't had time to process her boyfriend's murder — or her pregnancy — before the guilt of killing her friend was thrust upon her.

It would've been a hundred times worse if her parents hadn't taken care of the body that night. She'd probably be in jail right now if Dad wasn't a trained assassin. There was no way she could've gotten rid of the body, much less all that blood at the park. Then there was the matter of

Nate's car.

But now it was all taken care of. Dad was certain none of it would ever point to Hadley.

If only she could be so sure. And the guilt would stop eating at her.

She'd *killed* her friend.

The blood — so much of it — flooded her mind. The look of horror and shock on Nate's face as he realized what she'd done.

The dread that had washed through her.

Tears stung her eyes.

If there was ever a time she needed Duke back, it was now. But neither he nor Nate would ever return.

She blinked, and the tears spilled onto her face.

The first bell rang.

Hadley wiped the tears, checked her makeup, and hurried to the building. She'd barely have time to make it to her first class before the final bell.

She slid into her seat just in time.

The teacher may as well have been speaking Greek, as far as Hadley could understand. She rubbed her belly absentmindedly, but then stopped as soon as she realized what she was doing.

She was going to lose her mind soon if things didn't turn around. But how would they ever? Death couldn't be taken back. Duke was gone. Nate was gone.

Everyone around her put away their books and took out pencils.

Quiz time.

She swore under her breath and followed suit. For a moment, she couldn't remember what class she was in.

Mom shouldn't have made her come in today. It wasn't fair. Not with everything on her plate. Now she had to worry about Dad. What if he'd been caught for one of his killings? Maybe he'd made a mistake early on in his career, and it was catching up to him now.

She tried to force all those thoughts from her mind as soon as the kid in front of her set a stack of quizzes down on her desk. Hadley took one and passed the rest to the girl behind her.

It took a moment for her eyes to adjust the words. To recognize the letters as English. Understand the questions.

It was all stuff she already knew. She'd studied for this quiz over the weekend.

Relief washed through her.

Hadley was the second one to turn in her paper. And she was the only person to appreciate what a feat that was, considering everything plaguing her thoughts.

Somehow she managed to get through the rest of her morning classes without much effort. She even joined in a few conversations and made jokes, doing her best to give the impression that nothing was wrong.

Even though everything was.

By lunch, she'd even worked up an appetite. It was nice that food was no longer nauseating her. At least, not like it had been.

The pregnancy was progressing. Hadley really needed to figure out what she was going to do about the baby, besides having it. Like she'd told her parents, getting rid of it would be like losing Duke all over again.

That would kill her.

Now she was left with the biggest decision of her life. The thought of handing Duke's baby to a stranger didn't feel right. But she was hardly in a position to raise the baby, especially if she wanted to have a normal senior year.

Not that having a typical year was guaranteed without her child. Everything else in Hadley's life made it impossible. She was already falling down the social ladder rapidly.

She shoved those thoughts aside — none of that could be resolved at the moment — and grabbed some food before finding her friends at their regular table.

"Look who joined us." Ellie turned her nose up at Hadley.

The words from her best friend were like a knife to the heart.

Hadley swallowed and forced a weak smile. "I'm finally starting to feel better."

"Whatever." Ellie rolled her eyes before turning to her tray.

Everyone else at the table continued their conversations, laughing loudly, oblivious to the tension between the two friends.

Hadley's stomach sank, and her appetite waned. She tried saying something to Ellie, but with no response. Would Ellie ever forgive her for not telling her about Duke first? She wasn't sure if it would be better to apologize again or wait it out.

But when Ellie got up and huffed away, Hadley decided it might be time for another apology.

She stuffed the last few bites of mashed potatoes into her mouth before hurrying after her friend.

Ellie raced away from her, heading toward her locker.

Hadley caught up with her. "Ellie, I'm sorry. I mean it."

"For real?" Ellie crossed her arms. "You're sorry?"

"That's what I just said."

"You aren't really that dense, are you?"

Hadley blinked a few times. "Apparently I am."

"Look, if you can't figure it out, I'm sure not going to tell you."

"How does that help anything?"

15

Anger shone in Ellie's eyes. "I thought we were best friends."

"We *are*."

Ellie laughed bitterly. "Right. Leave me alone. You're good at that."

"Wait. Is this because I've been sick?"

"It's because you're a crappy best friend!"

"I can't help being sick! Plus, there's been a lot going on with my family. Not to mention the fact that my boyfriend is dead."

Ellie poked her shoulder, her face reddening. "The boyfriend you never told me about! I had to hear about him through gossip. Do you know how that made me feel?"

"I—"

"Forget it!" Ellie glowered at her. "I don't want to hear it. Leave me alone."

"No. We need to talk."

"It's almost time for class."

"I don't care. This is more important."

Ellie took a few steps back. "If it was really important to you, then you would have told me about Duke yourself — and before he was dead!"

Hadley drew in a shaky breath. "I couldn't tell anyone. He could've gotten into trouble because of our age difference."

"You could've told *me*. You just didn't trust me."

"But I promised him I wouldn't say anything to anyone. He could've gone to *jail*. We were going to tell people once I turned eighteen."

Ellie's nostrils flared. "You don't think I could've kept a secret?"

"I know you could have."

"And you still decided not to tell me. At least I know where I stand." Ellie walked away.

Hadley caught up. "It isn't like that!"

Ellie skidded to a stop and stared her down. "It's exactly like that. I'm done talking about this."

"Let me explain."

"No." She marched away.

The warning bell sounded.

Hadley threw her hands in the air and tried to swallow the lump in her throat. She hated that Ellie was furious with her, but she had to get to her next class. Besides, Hadley probably couldn't work things out with her until Ellie finally calmed down.

If she ever did.

Maybe losing her best friend was just one more loss to add to the year. And if that happened, she had no reason to stay at school. Well, other than to avoid looking like she was trying to hide something.

Hadley hurried to her locker, grabbed what she needed, and made her way to her next class.

Before she reached the door, a woman with a blue streak in her hair caught her attention.

The social worker who had been pestering her family about Nate's disappearance. She'd even been outside the house the previous night, when Dad had gotten arrested. Mom said she saw her among the neighbors.

Now she was back at school. Probably to question Hadley more.

People wouldn't stop talking about the fact that Nate and Hadley had been arguing at school before he disappeared. Nobody knew that he'd followed her all over town. Confronted her in the local park after she'd tried to lose him.

She couldn't say anything about that, though. Not without making herself look worse.

"Hadley!" The social worker waved as she hurried over.

Without a word, Hadley spun around and raced toward her class.

The psycho kept calling her.

Hadley's heart threatened to explode out of her chest. She raced inside the room and took her seat in the back, hiding behind the guy in front her but peeking around him out in the hall.

The woman was standing there, looking in.

She stayed there for the duration of the class, making it impossible for Hadley to focus. Not that she would've had an easy time even without her there.

The social worker — Jalinda or something — stayed right by the door for the whole hour. There would be no way for Hadley to avoid her when the bell rang.

That didn't stop her from trying. She waited until most of the other kids had made their way out and kids started coming in from the next class.

Jalinda didn't move.

Hadley clung to her bag, held her head high, and exited the classroom.

An arm grabbed her hand. "Hadley."

Hadley kept her gaze focused on the drinking fountain across the hallway. Marched as far as she could.

That woman held her in a steel grip.

Hadley turned to her and narrowed her eyes. "Do you mind?"

"I've been trying to talk to you."

"You know I'm not talking without a lawyer."

"I just have a few questions. Don't you care about Nate's safety?"

Guilt stung. Burned a hole in her heart. "Of course I do! But that doesn't mean I have anything to say to you. You need to let go of me. Now."

Jalinda loosened her grip, but didn't remove her hand. Held out a card. "If you think of anything that would help us find him, let me know. The family is getting desperate."

Hadley looked at the card. Jacinta Parks. Right. That was her name. Not that she cared. The nut was obsessed with her family.

"Will you do that?" she asked.

"Sure." Hadley stuffed the card into her bag. "I have to get to class."

Jacinta finally let go.

Hadley ran, her heart pounding.

Chapter Four

BRAD SHOVED his half-eaten lunch away. He was kind of hungry, despite his worries.

Faye should've contacted him by now, especially since the attorney hadn't shown up yet. She would know how much stress he'd be under.

What could possibly be going on outside these walls to keep her from letting him know what was going on? Was she trying to explain the situation to the lawyer? Were they trying to work around red tape?

Something had to be wrong.

His stomach churned acid at that thought. Made the gross meal feel like gravel in his gut.

Had he been set up to take the fall for one of the kills he'd taken on at work? The Bergmanns did have some of the evidence. And considering that Brad had figured out that Kurt was his dad's killer, there was nothing stopping them from trying to silence him. Death didn't work, so jail was the next best option. They'd put both Rose and Wes in jail without a second thought.

Why not Brad, too? All they had to do was threaten his family to keep him quiet.

Rage boiled. If they tried to touch any of them …

What? What could Brad do from inside a jail cell?

He leaped up, nearly tripping over his new roommate, who'd made the middle of the floor his space. He peered through the window.

The hall outside was empty. Officers rarely passed by unless they were bringing food. It wasn't a hall where they walked by to get anything else. Probably set up that way on purpose.

What if he had a medical emergency? Likely didn't matter — they were just criminals. So much for innocent until proven guilty. More like guilty until proven innocent. Except for the people he killed.

"What's got you so worked up?"

Brad jolted at the grainy voice of his roommate. He'd forgotten the guy was there.

The man sat cross-legged in the middle of the concrete floor, his hands resting on his knees like he was in some yoga class instead of a holding cell. "Well?"

"I need to get out of here. You don't?"

"I'll be released when the time is right." He closed his eyes, and his mouth formed an o-shape.

Brad shook his head and turned back to the window. Pounded on it in case anyone was near enough to hear anything.

"You think that'll help?"

"It's better than sitting around doing nothing."

He opened one eye. "I'm not *doing nothing*. I'm connecting with the universe."

Brad held back an eyeroll. "How's that working out for you?"

"Quite well. I'm making good progress."

"I'm sure you are." He turned back to the window and pounded. "Is anyone out there?"

"It's impossible to concentrate when you do that."

"Would you prefer I join you and meditate, too?"

The guy wrinkled his nose. "This isn't meditation. I'm connecting with the universe."

"And I'm trying to get out of here." Brad yelled again, hitting the window. Not that he expected much. People probably tried a lot worse on a regular basis to get the cops' attention.

He kept it up a few more minutes, ignoring the complaints of the yogi, before settling for pacing again.

"Do you really believe any of this will do any good?" His roommate tilted his head.

"It's no less effective than whatever you're doing."

"You're wrong there." He closed his eyes and muttered nonsense.

Brad shook his head and drew in a labored breath.

"Deep breathing. Wise."

"Glad to have your approval." Brad plopped onto his bed, forgetting how unforgiving it was, and ended up with sore seat bones.

His new friend continued his mumblings.

Brad focused on the window, ready to leap up at the slightest movement.

Nothing.

Time dragged on. He didn't even have a clock to watch the second hand move five times slower than it should.

Where was Faye? His attorney? How hard would it be to take just a few minutes to let him know what was going on? Even if they were working together outside the police station, it wouldn't be so difficult to let him in on the plan.

This was ridiculous. No, it was insanity.

There were rooms where they could talk. The police had to provide those legally. He was sure of it.

Keeping him in the dark was nothing other than maddening.

Everyone was hiding vital information from him — and this was his life on the line. What knife had they found? Where was it? Who had found it? Whose blood was on it? How sure were they that his prints were on it? Was it a BlueBlade knife? Some random brand?

And where was his attorney?

Brad leaped up, his skin hot. He clenched his fists and pounded hard enough to break normal glass.

His roommate said something.

Blood rushed in Brad's ears, blocking out whatever the other man had said. Helped him to focus on his anger and not get distracted by the woo-woo crap he was spouting.

Something brushed against his leg.

It was Mr. Woo-woo. He pointed to the window.

Detective Stewart stood on the other side.

He stared, thinking it was his imagination. A mirage, like a lake in the desert.

She waved Brad over.

Maybe she was a product of his thoughts.

He stumbled over, anyway. "I want to make my phone call now."

"Someone is here to speak with you."

"My attorney?"

"Her name is June Bancroft."

Brad gave her a double take. "Who?"

"June Bancroft."

He'd never heard the name. Perhaps she was an attorney who worked with his. Or maybe the Bergmanns had sent her to scare him. "Did she say what she wants?"

"To talk with you. Would you prefer I send her away?"

STACY CLAFLIN & NOLON KING

"No," Brad quickly replied.

His breathing was ragged as the detective led him down the hallway. Would the woman waiting for him help him or threaten his family?

Detective Stewart stopped at a closed door, knocked, then opened it. Shoved him inside.

The waiting woman rose from her seat. She was tall and slender with long straight black hair and matching eyes. June Bancroft wore a smart suit and an unreadable expression.

Only one thing was certain.

He'd never seen this woman before in his life.

Chapter Five

BRAD STUDIED the mysterious woman as Detective Stewart cuffed him to the table.

She left, and then it was just Brad with the woman who would either help or make his situation all the worse.

They stared each other down.

It could go either way.

"Who are you?" he finally asked.

She straightened her back and stared him down. "I'm Agent June Bancroft."

"Agent?"

"Correct." She didn't avert or soften her glare.

"And you're here because …?"

"I believe we can help each other."

Brad nearly laughed, but managed to keep his expression stoic. "Help each other how?"

"You have access to information I need, and I can get you out of here."

He tilted his head. "You have my attention."

She pulled out an electronic tablet and slid her finger around the screen.

Brad's mind raced as he tried to figure out what was going on. Was she with the FBI? Did she work for a secret agency, like he did, but unlike him got a fancy title? For all the good his secret agency and his top secret security clearance were doing him now.

Agent Bancroft continued her scrolling for a solid three minutes.

Felt like an hour.

Then she finally turned back to him. Didn't say anything.

"What's going on?" Brad demanded. "The police won't tell me anything. All I know is that supposedly there's a bloody knife with my prints on it. The attorney I told my wife to call hasn't shown up, and I haven't heard from her, either. And now here you are. None of this makes sense. I deserve to know what's going on!"

She nodded. "I agree. But you don't need an attorney now that I'm here."

"How can you get me out? You posting my bail?"

"No." She leaned forward. "Before I do anything, I need to know you'll help me."

"With what, exactly?"

She drew a slow breath that seemed more for dramatic effect than anything else. "You work for Kurt Bergmann, is that right?"

"Yes. I'm sure you already know all about that."

"And BlueBlade is more than it appears?"

"Right."

"You're more than a manager at a knife store. More than a traveling salesman."

"What agency did you say you're with?" Brad asked.

"I didn't."

"I know."

26

One side of her mouth curved up slightly. "Does the name Callum Forsythe mean anything to you?"

Brad's breath hitched. Forsythe was one of the targets Brad had killed last year. One of the few he'd traveled all the way to Europe to take out.

Agent Bancroft lifted a brow. "Is that a yes?"

"I'm aware of Callum Forsythe."

"I assume you know where he's located?"

Meaning his body.

Affirming her meant admitting his guilt.

And she could've been toying with him. Looking to take him down for Callum's death. Then there would be more reason for his being in prison. Although technically, only travel could get him tried for that particular killing. Not that there was any evidence without him providing *details* of the body's location. If it hadn't fully disintegrated by now. That could go either way.

"Well?" Agent Bancroft tapped her mahogany-colored nails on the table.

"I can account for where I last saw him, yes."

"Good." She listed off several other names, insisting that Brad confirm knowledge of the bodies and their locations.

He did.

"What does any of this have to do with my freedom?" Brad asked.

"These details need to be acknowledged prior to any help I can provide."

He frowned, but then quickly hid his emotion. "Are you sufficiently convinced?"

She studied him, her gaze seeming to bore into his soul. "Yes, I believe so. Now the question is, are you willing to help me?"

"You say you're able to get me out of here?"

"Free and clear."

He blinked a few times. "You're talking immunity?"

"I'm talking *full* immunity."

"Full?"

It was an odd offer, considering his innocence. Immunity was saved for the guilty. Did she think he needed immunity for killing his government-sanctioned targets? Brad didn't need to be pardoned for the deaths of Callum Forsythe and the like.

Yes, he was always careful to destroy evidence and leave nothing behind, but that was only because they weren't to draw attention to the local authorities who couldn't know anything about their organization.

They were above law enforcement.

He decided that he would worry about that once he was out of here and able to take matters into his own hands.

"I clearly know about your" — Bancroft cleared her throat — "business dealings. I have record of more."

Brad's stomach knotted. How much did she know?

"Well? I don't have all day."

"Why me? And what exactly do you want from me?"

"You can get close to Kurt Bergmann."

That would be tricky, but he wasn't about to admit it. Not if she could get him out of this place. "I can."

She made a note on her tablet.

"What exactly do you want from me?"

"I need information he keeps locked in either his office or his home. Possibly somewhere else."

That made the situation exponentially trickier. But he nodded as if it didn't. "Okay."

"It could mean skirting the law."

Brad glanced around for cameras.

"This room is safe," Agent Bancroft assured him.

He cleared his throat. "I can work with those parameters. And in exchange, you're offering me full immunity?"

She nodded. "Correct. And you'll be free and clear, not obligated to continue working with BlueBlade any longer."

Now it was sounding too good to be true. "What's the catch?"

"Only that I need the information and both Bergmanns alive."

Brad wouldn't be able to kill his father's murderer.

But he could turn him over. Perhaps then he might receive a fate worse than death.

That would still be satisfying.

"And I get to walk out of here a free man?"

"Yes. Assuming you get me what I want."

"If I don't?"

Her expression stiffened. "That isn't an option. Understood?"

"Understood."

"Great." She turned back to her tablet. "I have some details to work out. For now, you'll return to the holding cell."

He thought of his roommate. "Not here? I can answer more questions about those people you were asking about."

She shook her head, her attention still on the screen. "I have some calls to make."

"How long until I can go home?"

The agent glanced back at him. "You won't be going straight home. There's still plenty for you and I to discuss."

She got up and called for an officer before he could respond.

Two minutes later he was back in the cell with Mr. Meditation. Brad ignored him and went back to the mattress he'd slept on the night before.

Was this really happening? Instead of going to prison for life, was he actually going to be set free?

The word *immunity* still nagged at him.

He'd always assumed that if he were ever caught, Kurt would contact the appropriate higher-ups and have him released, shut down the case. But now that he knew Kurt was the enemy, that wasn't going to happen. And who the higher-ups were — the ones who issued their security clearances — was kept secret. Because the government didn't want low-level assassins blabbing evidence of their highly classified bureau to the cops. Or the press. Or anyone else.

The fact that Brad was still sitting in a holding cell made him wonder if Kurt had made those higher-ups see him as rogue. Thought he needed "retirement" as a danger to the program.

In which case, Bancroft was his only hope of remaining a free man.

She might not be any more trustworthy than the Bergmanns. But at least she could get him out of the police station. Once free, he could figure the rest of it out. Force Kurt to tell him what he'd done, and who Brad needed to talk to in order to clear his name with the higher-ups.

He watched the window. Time seemed to move slower than ever. But at least progress was being made. Every moment that passed, no matter how sluggishly, brought him closer to home. Even if he had to spend several hours hashing out details with the agent, at least he would be on the other side of these walls.

Brad was so lost in thought he'd forgotten about his roommate. It startled him when the other man stood to use the toilet.

Where was Agent Bancroft?

He got up and looked out the window. As much as he

tried to ignore his roommate, he couldn't. No matter how he stood, the yogi's reflection caught on the glass.

Then finally, movement out in the hallway.

Brad craned his neck to see who was coming his way.

Detective Stewart, and she didn't look happy.

Agent June Bancroft walked alongside her.

Brad was about to become a free man.

He hoped.

Chapter Six

FAYE GLANCED OVER AT DIANNE, who was chatting with a customer in the waiting room. Talking about her new haircut from the looks of it, since she kept touching her hair and pointing toward Faye.

At least she wasn't bored. Although, it was only a matter of time. Depending on how long it took Brad to get out of the jail, Faye would either have to continue bringing her mother-in-law into work with her or find someone else to stay home with her.

Or quit early. She had a salon at home ready and waiting. And she was going into business for herself, so it wasn't like she would have to explain in a job interview why she'd quit abruptly after giving two weeks' notice.

Faye did her best to keep her mind on the task at hand. It was a simple trim, nothing fancy. But her next client was a lady who routinely got complicated perms with different curl patterns and colors for each layer. She needed to pull herself together in the next twenty minutes.

That was a lot to ask, but she could do it. She'd managed to get through the day with everything else that had been going on all year. Or at least it felt like one entire calendar year. Duke was killed before his big Super Bowl party not that long ago, but every day felt like a week, and every week like a month.

Hopefully it would all turn around soon. Though they still had to wait out Hadley's pregnancy. It was crazy that she wanted to keep it, though Faye could see the reasoning behind her sentimentality. It was just that Hadley was only seventeen — she had no idea the havoc a full-term pregnancy would wreak on her body, leaving marks that would never go away. And that didn't even touch the emotional hell she'd go through.

With any luck, her daughter would have the sense to give the baby up for adoption. Faye and Brad sure weren't going to raise it. They were *done*.

The thought jolted her. What if Brad didn't get out of jail? If the lawyer couldn't work her magic, then Brad might spend the rest of his life in prison. Or worse. She had no idea if their state had the death penalty.

Surely the secret government agency he worked for would make sure he wasn't executed for doing the work they'd hired him to do.

Or was that how they remained a secret agency — by disavowing any employee who got caught?

What if they were going to hang Brad out to dry, to protect themselves?

"Are you okay?"

Faye blinked a few times, bringing herself back to the salon.

"Faye?" Her client stared at her with concern in her eyes.

"Yeah, sorry. Got lost in thought for a moment." Faye shook her head to clear it. "You were telling me about your son's soccer tournament?"

Cindy nodded and continued with her story.

Faye silently chastised herself. She needed to either pull herself together or take the rest of the day off. This wasn't a job where she could be halfway there mentally. One wrong snip could mean months of bad hair days for someone.

Maybe she shouldn't have listened to Kurt. It was too much to try and focus while her husband was under arrest for a murder he didn't commit.

Or did he?

She shoved the thought aside and focused on the trim, trying to listen to the story about the soccer game.

Tears threatened at the thought of Brad staying behind bars permanently. She blinked them back and tried to focus.

Maybe taking the rest of the day off would be her best option. Especially with the complicated hairstyle coming up. She needed to be at the top of her game for that.

She glanced at the clock. It was after one — almost her lunch time. Past when most people ate. Had Brad eaten already? Or was he so miserable that he'd been refusing his food? Whatever he'd been offered probably wasn't appealing. She'd need to come up with a delicious and healthy meal to welcome him back with after his release.

If he was released.

No. When. There would be no *if*.

Next to the scissors underneath the mirror plastered with photos of her family, her cell phone rang.

Her heart stopped.

She'd silenced her phone, only allowing in calls from Brad or his attorney's number.

"Do you need to get that?" Cindy asked.

Faye stared at it, lighting up again. "I … uh … I'm not supposed take it when with a client."

"Something is obviously going on. Your mind is else-where, sweetie. Please, take it."

She looked back and forth between her almost-done client and the phone. Then she leaped over and snatched it up.

Brad. That could only mean one thing. He'd been released and got his phone back.

Unless something bad had happened, and someone was using his phone to notify her?

"Answer it," Cindy urged.

Faye swallowed and accepted the call. Her shaky finger nearly rejected the call. She raised it to her ear. "Brad?"

Her throat nearly closed, as she expected to hear another voice deliver more bad news.

She wasn't sure she could take it.

"It's me."

Her knees turned to rubber. She leaned against the counter for support. "Are you … you're out already?"

"I am. It's a really long story, but I just stepped out into freedom."

She released a breath. "I can't believe it! Do you need me to pick you up? Or are they driving you back home?"

"I have a ride. It's a little complicated."

"What is?" She wanted to ask if it was about bail, but didn't dare say it out loud for all her coworkers and her client to hear.

"I'll explain at home tonight. But I do have a question — what happened with the attorney?"

"I couldn't reach her."

"So, you didn't send anyone? Or call me to let me know what was going on?"

"What are you talking about?" She tried to make sense of what he was saying. "Kurt sent his."

"Kurt?"

"Yeah. Last night."

"He didn't."

The words were a slap. "I called him after I couldn't reach anyone at the number you gave me. He promised he'd take care of it."

Brad muttered something.

"What?" she asked.

"He's the one behind my arrest. I'm sure of it. We can't trust the Bergmanns — either of them."

"You really think so?"

"I know so. I've got—"

"Wait. How did you …?" She couldn't find an unsuspicious way to finish her sentence.

"Luckily, someone was watching out for me. I can't explain it over the phone. Tonight."

Faye excused herself to Cindy and hurried outside, where she could speak in private. "I did my best! Your lawyer didn't answer, and I kept on calling. Once it became clear that she wouldn't be any help, I called Kurt. He did so much for my salon, I figured he could work some magic for your situation, too."

"We can't trust them farther than we can throw Ralf's Bentley."

"How'd you get out, if not for Kurt's lawyer?"

"Like I said, I can't say over the phone."

"I'm outside. Nobody from work will hear anything."

"It's not that. The phone could be tapped. I've probably already said more than I should."

Faye sighed. "Can you tell me *something*?"

"I'm out, I'm not going back in. I'll be home tonight."

"That hardly tells me anything."

"If you're at work, where's my mom?"

"She's here with me. Kurt said to carry on with life as usual, because he would take care of everything."

"Of course he did." Brad's tone was strained.

"I didn't know he was lying. I'd have—"

"It's fine. I have to go."

"When are you getting home?"

"I don't know exactly. Love you."

"You too."

The call ended.

She tried to wrap her mind around everything he'd said. Not that he'd given much to go on. If he didn't have an attorney, how did he get out? And what was he doing that he couldn't discuss over the phone?

Acid churned in her stomach.

But he was out of jail. That was all that mattered. Or at the very least, that was what she needed to focus on. Despite all the unanswered questions, he would be home that night. Maybe even by the time she got off work.

Faye hurried inside, whispering the good news to Dianne before returning to her client. She looked around, almost wanting someone to dare confront her about taking a call during a haircut.

Nobody did.

At least she was able to finish up with Cindy, who gave her a generous tip.

Faye's next client was already waiting, glancing at the clock every few minutes.

After Faye swept the floor under her chair and counter, she hurried to the back room and collapsed onto a couch. Who knew what Brad's freedom might entail, but at least he was coming home.

Maybe, just maybe, they could carry on with their lives as if the awful arrest hadn't happened.

Chapter Seven

"NICE OFFICE." Brad sat at the empty table in the middle of the equally-empty room.

Agent Bancroft didn't so much as crack a smile.

No sense of humor. Note taken. He leaned back and appreciated how much cushier the chair was than that joke of a mattress in his holding cell.

Bancroft opened a manila file and spread out some papers before pulling her hair into a tight ponytail. She glanced over some of them before turning to Brad. "How close are you to your boss?"

"Depends on what you mean by close."

"Can you get into his office?"

"Not unsupervised."

"His house?"

"Again, not without prying eyes."

"Will he tell you privileged information?"

"Not likely."

The agent frowned deeply.

"Once I warm him up, sure."

"Good. I'm going to set you up with a wire. It might be

quicker to get him talking than to find the paperwork I need."

"Whatever you need me to do."

She flipped through a few more of these papers. "Tell me what you know about the company."

"BlueBlade?"

"The real organization. The assassination operation. From what I've gathered, you're one of the senior assassins."

"I am." He drew in a deep breath.

"So, you know more than most of the others."

"Yes. I joined after the market crash. Moved up the ranks fairly quickly and spent a good deal of time training the newbies."

"So, Kurt trusts you."

Brad held back a scowl. "The man has tried to kill me and has set me up for three murders I didn't commit. No, I don't think he trusts me."

"He tried to kill you?"

"I've been attacked when on missions. The only reason I wasn't last time was because I didn't let Kurt know what I was doing. He was pissed that the target was actually taken out. That confirmed his involvement in the ambushes."

Bancroft shook her head. "Those were our people."

He stared in disbelief. "What?"

"You've been encroaching on our territory."

Brad leaped to his feet, sending the wheeled chair flying behind him. "You get me out of jail to tell me that *you* were behind the hits on my life?"

She wrinkled her nose. "Nobody was trying to kill you. Sit down."

"Like hell I will."

Bancroft furrowed her brows. "We were trying to *capture* you. Big difference."

"Capture. Kill. Pretty much the same thing." He glowered at her.

"Sit."

"No."

They stared each other down.

Bancroft tucked a loose strand of hair behind her ear. "I've had the same goal this entire time — and at no point has it had anything to do with your demise."

"What, then?"

She panned her palms around the room. "To get you in here."

"Why?"

"If you'll have a seat, I'll explain."

"Fine. But only because I need to hear your explanation."

"And because I can offer you immunity."

"For a crime I didn't commit." He grabbed the chair and sat with gusto.

"You mean for a string of murders you *have been* committing around the world for more than a decade."

"They weren't murders."

Bancroft tilted her head. "What were they, then?"

"Government-sanctioned killings of criminals who have escaped justice of the law."

She snorted. "Is that what they've been telling you?"

"What's so funny about that?"

"You think you work for the government? For the good guys?"

"I've been making this world a safer place."

The agent rubbed her forehead. "This is going to be a lot more work than I thought."

"What are you talking about?"

"This is going to take deprogramming."

It was his turn to snort. "Deprogramming?"

"Yes."

"You make it sound like I've been in a cult."

"That's not too far off the mark."

"What are you talking about?"

The agent pressed her palms on the table and leaned forward. "You don't work for a government agency, Mr. Morris. BlueBlade is covering an *illegal* operation that services organized crime and some of the most corrupt governments in the world. You work for the bad guys."

Brad could barely breathe. "You're wrong."

"I've been tracking your people for years."

The room seemed to spin around him. "What are you saying?"

"You're no idiot. You know exactly what I'm saying."

Brad closed his eyes and rubbed his temples, pulse drumming in his ears. "Have I been killing innocent people?"

He didn't want to know the answer.

"Not innocent, but also probably not the criminals you've been told you were taking out. What did they tell you?"

Brad let the news sink in a moment before looking at her. "I thought I was taking out hardened criminals — the worst of the worst, who had gotten away with heinous crimes. I was supposed to be making the world a safer place."

Silence hung between them.

"What have I really been doing?"

"The short answer is that the Bergmanns have actually been making kills to manipulate the politics of powerful foreign and domestic companies."

"Companies? Why?"

"Money is power. Taking out these people brings your bosses more power."

Brad slumped down in his chair. "I had no idea. Really, I believed it was part of a legitimate government agency."

"Unfortunately not. Your actions have led to the manipulation of more than the politics of companies. We're talking about political ramifications worldwide."

Brad swore.

Her expression softened. "By working with me you can make things right. We can take down the Bergmanns and their entire empire."

His heart thundered. "How do I know I can trust you?"

"Want to see my identification?"

He just stared.

"Did you ever see proof of the Bergmanns working for a government agency?"

"I can't remember." He should've been more thorough. But because of his financial troubles, Brad had blindly accepted the word of his friend.

Stupid. He'd been so, so stupid.

"Don't feel bad. I'm sure their IDs were convincing. I've seen a few near perfect forgeries."

Bancroft slid over a badge.

She was CIA. If she could be believed.

If anyone could be.

He didn't know what was real.

It wouldn't surprise him to see a unicorn walk in and offer him a cup of coffee.

"How do I know you're really CIA?"

"I got you out of jail, didn't I? Your charges are being cleared as we speak, if the process isn't already done."

He drew in a deep breath. "So, what now?"

She took back her ID and leaned forward. "You go back to work as if nothing is wrong. Get as close to Kurt as possible. Gain his trust — get into his office and his house. Find what you can on the company. That's what I need."

Brad tugged on his hair. Kurt would be the last person to trust him. He'd killed Brad's dad, and he knew Brad was looking into it. He just couldn't be sure if Brad knew the truth.

"Is there a problem?" Agent Bancroft asked.

"How will he trust me?"

"Because you're one of his longest-standing assassins."

"He had me framed for murder! Three separate times."

She lifted a brow. "Weren't the first two orchestrated by Rose Flores and Wes Campbell?"

"You've done your homework."

"We wouldn't be here otherwise."

"He was behind those hits on me. Unless you did that, too."

"That wasn't us."

His mind was spinning. "And now I'm supposed to trust you."

"Do you have another option?"

She had him there.

"If I help you take down the Bergmanns, then I get full immunity."

"Correct."

He drew a deep breath. "What about the other operation?"

"Which one? I'm following a complicated web of assassinations."

"The one behind the Slippery Fish car wash."

"Yes, that's one of them. Wes Campbell was part of that for years."

Brad closed his eyes. This whole thing was insanity. He half-expected to find himself back in the holding cell when he opened his eyes.

He was still in the office, and Agent Bancroft was looking at him as if expecting him to say something.

"What's the connection between us and them? And is the Slippery Fish legit?"

"No."

His stomach knotted, then lurched.

That meant his dad had also been killing people illegally.

Did he know that? Or had he also been under the illusion of working for a legitimate government agency?

"Do you have any other questions?" she asked.

"How about, where is the nearest toilet, so I can puke?"

"Do you really need a bathroom?"

"No." He tugged on his collar. "What's the plan? How do I get started?"

She turned to her tablet and moved her finger around the screen before answering. "Go into work tomorrow like everything is normal. Don't look at or play with the wires. You'd be surprised how many people give themselves away by doing that."

"I'm a professional."

"Good. When Bergmann is shocked to see you — and he no doubt will be — pretend not to notice. Act like nothing has changed. Be his buddy."

"*That* isn't typical."

"Then *make* it work."

He swallowed. "Okay."

"Do everything in your power to regain his trust. I don't care what it takes."

That would be tough if Kurt had the faintest suspicion that Brad had been talking to anyone in law enforcement. "What do I tell him when he asks how I got out of jail?"

"Whatever he'll believe."

"What if he gives me a new target?"

"Then take the job."

"You want me to kill an innocent person?"

She shook her head. "I didn't say *complete* the job. Bring it to me."

"And then?"

"Tell him you're working on it. I'll deal with the rest."

"He'll know that it isn't taken care of."

"Let me worry about that."

Brad frowned.

The agent leaned forward. "You need to get it through your head that I'm your new boss. You report to me. Hourly, if necessary. That, and becoming Kurt Bergmann's new BFF, is your only concern. Everything else is on me. Got it?"

"Understood."

His life had just gotten exponentially more complicated.

Chapter Eight

Brad stepped out of Agent Bancroft's car and closed the door. Barely noticed the vehicle leaving. Stared at his house. It felt like years since he'd last seen it. Yet at the same time, the memories of his family and neighbors watching his arrest felt like only moments ago.

All he wanted to do was sleep, but he needed to explain everything to Faye first.

That would be no small task. Everything he'd learned from the agent had been shocking, so he could only imagine how hard it would be for his civilian wife to hear. At least he'd already opened up to her about him being an assassin. That was one less thing to worry about. This conversation would be intolerably complicated if she didn't already know about that.

The stares of curious neighbors burned on his back. Ignoring the temptation to give them all the one-finger salute, he stood tall and marched into the house, taking his sweet time. Now they could whisper about him being a free man. Not nearly as exciting as another arrest in the neighborhood, but it would do. And it put him in a good light.

Once at the door, he dug into his pockets. No keys. Right. He hadn't had them on him at the time of his arrest.

Still feeling the watchful eyes, he rang the bell. His cheeks warmed slightly, but really he didn't care what those nosy bastards thought. He couldn't wait to have conversations with them and stare them directly in the eye as they questioned him in person, as they undoubtedly would.

Footsteps thundered, and the door flung open. Luna appeared on the other side.

"Daddy!" She flung her arms around his waist.

He pulled her into his arms, hugging her tightly as he stepped inside and closed the door behind them, shutting out the world and its prying eyes.

"I missed you!" Luna buried her face into his neck.

"And I missed you."

Conversation sounded from the kitchen. He headed in there with Luna still clinging to him.

His mom and wife joined the embrace, eagerly welcoming him back.

It felt great to be home again, able to wrap his arms around his family. He would never take that for granted again.

After a minute, he stepped back and set Luna down. "Are Hadley and Zeke upstairs?"

"Yes," his mom said, smiling. "Let them know you're back. Faye and I are almost done with dinner."

Brad brought his hands to his stomach. "I'm famished."

"I'm sure you are. We're making my famous pot roast. It always was your favorite." She rested her hand on his arm.

He kissed her cheek and headed upstairs.

Faye quickly caught up with him and slid her fingers

through his. "Was it horrible? Like what we see on TV? Did anyone threaten you? Start a fight?"

He shook his head. "It was just a holding cell in a suburban police station — a lot of concrete and a paper-thin mattress with zero privacy."

"So, no thugs giving you a hard time?"

"My roommate spent most of his time meditating on the floor. It was easy enough to ignore him."

Relief flooded her expression. "Oh, good. I was so worried."

He squeezed her hand. "I'd have been fine in a prison, though. I can handle myself."

"How'd you manage to get out, if Kurt never sent a lawyer to help you?"

"It's a long story. Let me see the kids, and then I'll explain."

"I hope you have time before the roast is ready."

"At the very least, I'll give you the short version." He found both the teenagers in their respective rooms, and their hugs were every bit as enthusiastic as the ones downstairs.

Once in the master bedroom, he eagerly got out of his clothes and took a quick shower while telling Faye about waiting for his attorney and meeting Agent Bancroft. She asked a lot of questions while Brad let the hot water massage his sore muscles.

After he changed into sweats and a T-shirt, Faye glanced at the door. "I want to hear the rest, but I really should check on your mom. She might need help with something, even though she says she can handle it all."

"I'll send Zeke down." Brad sent their son a text, and once he had confirmation that he was going down to the kitchen, Brad resumed his story.

Faye rubbed circles on his palms and listened with wide eyes while Brad explained his deal with Bancroft.

"You really think she's legit?"

"I'm no expert on verifying CIA badges, but she appears to be the real deal. She knows all about the Bergmanns, and most of my assigned targets."

She swallowed. "The people you killed?"

Brad nodded.

"And they were actually innocent?"

"No, but they also weren't the hardened criminals I believed I was taking out. I was interfering with company politics, and in some cases, actual politics."

Faye paled. "Illegally?"

Guilt stabbed him as he nodded in confirmation. He took her hands in his. "I'm so sorry, Faye. If I'd had any idea, I never would've gotten involved. Not a chance. I would never do anything to put you or the kids in danger. I truly believed that I was doing the right thing, making the world a safer place."

She sighed. "You had no reason to think Kurt was lying."

"Still, I should've done more research. But in my idiotic desperation, I believed too easily. If I could only go back in time …"

"But you can't. All we can do is make the best of the situation we're in now."

His heart warmed, and he pulled her close. "Thank you for being so understanding. I screwed up big time."

"Now you have the opportunity to make it all right. And you said that means trying to get some information from Kurt?"

Brad brushed some of her hair aside and kissed her temple. "Yes. I have to go back to work and act like everything is hunky-dory. Somehow convince that bastard that I'm not onto him about anything."

"That means we have to figure who can watch your mom during the day. Kurt did mention something about hiring a day nurse if we needed the help."

"I don't want to rely on anyone he sends." Brad scowled at the thought. "Agent Bancroft said she would set something up. Said she knew of some adult daycares."

"Dianne's going to love that."

"Actually, she might. From what the agent said, they provide not only socialization but opportunities for games, crafts, and other activities. Sounds like something Mom would enjoy."

Faye didn't look convinced. "When do you go back to BlueBlade?"

"She wants me to go in tomorrow. She's supposed to text me the details."

"And you get full immunity for everything if you do this?"

"That's what she says."

Faye leaned back and sighed. "You don't sound convinced."

"I have my doubts about getting close enough to Kurt to find anything useful. He's going to trust me about as much as a snake."

She frowned.

"I might have to get some acting tips from Hadley if I'm going to convince him that I've had a change of heart."

Knock, knock!

"Dinner's ready," Zeke called from the other side of the door.

Faye got up and cracked open the door. "Thanks,

sweetie. We'll be down in just a sec." She closed the door and turned back to Brad. "Ready?"

His stomach rumbled, but his nerves were shot. He could do a lot of things, but convince Kurt he didn't want to throttle him? That would be a challenge of the highest order.

Faye sat and rested a hand on his knee. "Something else on your mind?"

"All I want is to kill Kurt. Do you have any idea how difficult it's going to be to act like his friend?"

"Just think about how pretending will lead to his arrest. That should help, I would think."

"I don't want him in prison — I want him dead!" Brad squeezed his fists. "He killed my dad!"

Faye gasped. "What?"

Brad closed his eyes momentarily. "With everything else going on, I didn't get a chance to tell you. When I was going through Dad's old journals, he wrote about it. He thought Kurt was going to attack him."

Faye covered her mouth. "You're sure it was the same Kurt?"

"Do you know another Kurt Bergmann?"

"How did your dad know him?"

"The real question is, how did I end up working for Kurt when he was the one who murdered my dad?"

"But you don't know that for sure."

"It's too much of a coincidence. It was him."

Knock, knock!

"You guys coming?" Zeke called.

"Yes!" Brad said.

Faye stared at him, wide-eyed. "You aren't thinking of killing him, are you?"

"He deserves nothing less."

"But prison will be punishment enough, won't it?"

STACY CLAFLIN & NOLON KING

"It isn't as bad as the son of one of his victims killing *him*. That's justice. Especially after pulling me into this business and pretending like he had no idea about my dad's death."

She clung to him. "But will you get immunity for killing Kurt? It sounds like that agent wants him alive."

"She does, and no, there's no immunity agreement if I kill him. But if it happens, it happens. Bancroft will understand."

"But will the police? Are you really going to try to do it yourself?"

"If I'm given the opportunity, I'll take it without a second thought."

Faye's eyes flooded with concern. "Please reconsider."

"I've been looking for my father's murderer for three decades. Now he's within my reach. He's going to pay with his life."

Chapter Nine

HADLEY SCARFED DOWN the roast and potatoes like she'd never seen food before. She hadn't been hungry until piling the food on her plate. Her nerves had stolen her appetite, between her worries about Dad's arrest and Ellie being pissed at her.

At least one of those problems had been solved.

She didn't know what to do about Ellie, but part of her didn't care. If her friend was more concerned about the fact that she'd kept a secret than she was about how Hadley was doing, then maybe she wasn't that great a friend to begin with.

Hadley obviously didn't have the best taste in friends, given that she'd picked both Ellie and Nate. Or maybe the people that hung around her only cared about popularity, and that was something that came easy to her.

"Are you okay, honey?" Grandma placed a hand on Hadley's arm and gave her a concerned smile.

"Just tired." Hadley tried to return the smile. "I've been worried about Dad."

At least that much was true.

Grandma nodded. "We all have."

Zeke took another piece of roast. "What was jail like, Dad?"

"It wasn't really a jail. Just a holding cell."

"So, nothing like the movies?"

"Nope."

"Bummer. I mean, I guess that's good."

Hadley shot him a glare.

"What?"

"Why'd you have to go there, Daddy?" Luna asked.

"It was all a misunderstanding," Mom said quickly. She always sheltered Luna. They all did, really. Living in this family, the kid needed it. "That's why he's back home now. Because he didn't do anything wrong."

Luna nodded and turned back to her plate, obviously satisfied with that answer. Oh, to be seven again. Life was so much simpler, before friendships got complicated and people threw around threats. Before she'd felt the need to carry a knife for protection.

Zeke gulped down his milk and turned to Dad. "So, you didn't need to make a shank to defend yourself?"

"Zeke!" Mom glared at him.

"It's a valid question."

"This isn't dinner table talk."

"It is for this family."

"Zeke."

"Fine."

Hadley sighed dramatically, but she was glad for the distraction. She didn't want to think about Ellie, and she really didn't want to think about Nate. But the images of his blank eyes and bloody everything kept pushing their way to the front of her mind no matter what she was doing. It seemed to be getting worse rather than better. But not much time had passed, and people were still looking for him. Maybe once everyone moved on, her conscience would give her a break.

Or maybe she needed to talk to Dad and find out how he dealt with the guilt. Granted, he'd never killed one of his friends, but somehow he'd learned how to live with the knowledge that he'd taken a lot of lives. Sure, they were people that deserved death, but it still had to impact his psyche. At least at the beginning. And he had told her she could talk to him about it.

She probably needed to stop trying to handle it all on her own and ask him. Sometimes it seemed like her parents were totally clueless, but this was Dad's domain. He was one of the few people who understood.

Ding-dong!

Hadley dropped her fork, her blood running cold.

She exchanged a worried look with Zeke. He seemed to be thinking the same thing — that the police were back for dad.

Or maybe they were here for her this time.

What if they'd found out she'd killed Nate?

Luna ran over to their parents, tears running down her face. "Is it the police again, Daddy?"

"It shouldn't be. I was cleared."

"What does that mean?"

Mom pulled Luna to her lap. "It means the police made a mistake last night."

Zeke leaped up and ran to the window. "I don't see any police cars outside."

"Any cars?" Mom asked.

"A red one. Looks old and beat up. Not the kind that's usually parked around here." He craned his neck. "I can't see the porch. I don't know who it is."

Hadley's heart hammered. "It's not that social worker, is it?"

Dad whipped his head toward her. "She hasn't been following you kids again, has she?"

"She was at school today. I told her to leave me alone, unless I had a lawyer. Not that she doesn't already know that."

His face contorted and he slapped the table, making Luna jump in Mom's lap. He pushed the chair back. "I'm going to deal with this, then find out what the agent has to say about it."

Mom's eyes nearly bulged out of her head. "Should we bring that up with her?"

Ding-dong!

Dad frowned. "I can be judicious with the details I share. In the meantime, I'm going to put a stop to this."

Hadley looked back and forth between them. "What agent are you talking about?"

"Never mind." Dad raced out of the kitchen.

Hadley leaped up.

"Sit," Mom ordered.

"But—"

"I don't want you anywhere near the front door." She set Luna down, then told Hadley and Zeke, "You two stay here. I'm serious."

Then she hurried out of the room.

Hadley sat on her shaking hands.

"Who do you think it is?" Zeke asked.

"I'm going to find out. You stay here."

Grandma put a hand up. "Your parents said to stay here."

"I won't leave the kitchen." Hadley crept toward the hall and peeked around the corner.

Mom and Dad were standing at the door, blocking her view of who stood outside. She cupped her ear to try and hear what they were saying.

Dad apologized and said he didn't know where someone was — probably Nate. Who else would anyone be looking for?

Hadley inched closer until she was completely in the hallway, except for one foot.

"Hadley," Grandma whispered.

She held up a finger and tried to hear.

"I wish we could help you," Dad said, "but we haven't seen him. Best of luck to you."

Mom said something that Hadley couldn't make out, then closed the door. Then her parents turned around, both of them looking annoyed to see her standing there.

"I told you to stay in the kitchen."

Hadley pointed to her foot. "Who was that?"

Dad straightened his back. "Let's just finish dinner."

"Who *was* that?"

They exchanged a look.

"You know I'm going to keep asking until you tell me." Hadley folded her arms.

"That was Nate's biological mom," Dad said.

The floor dropped beneath her feet. Hadley grabbed for the wall. "What?"

"She heard about the search for him — that he was looking for her — and now she's joining the efforts to find him."

Hadley swore.

"No bad words," Luna said behind her.

"This is never going to end." Pain stabbed Hadley's temples.

Mom rested a hand on her shoulder. "Let us handle it."

"But you guys are dealing with Dad's stuff. He probably still has to go to court, doesn't he? Isn't that how it works?"

"His charges were dropped, so we can focus on your problems."

Dad embraced her and whispered, "And nobody's going to find Nate."

Hadley nodded, but she wouldn't be convinced until everyone stopped looking.

But now his real mom wanted to find him. His real dad could join in, too. Soon it would be the whole world.

Someone would find something.

"Come eat, Hadley," Grandma said

She pulled herself from her thoughts and realized she was the only one not at the table. "I'm done eating. I need to do homework."

Hadley ran upstairs before anyone could object. It was her night to do dishes, but she didn't care. Nobody else likely would either, given all the family drama.

She plopped down on her bed and absentmindedly rubbed her stomach as she thought about Nate's mom — who he would never get to meet, thanks to Hadley.

Tears welled in her eyes, and the ever-present lump swelled in her throat. This was never going to go away, even if people *did* stop looking for Nate. Nothing would change the fact that he was dead, and she had killed him. She'd stolen everything from him — his chance to grow up and have a family, to meet his birth parents, do anything at all.

It was all her fault.

She didn't bother wiping her tears away.

Knock, knock.

"Go away!"

"It's me, sweetheart."

Dad.

"I said, go away."

"I'm coming in, so you better cover up if you're not dressed."

She sighed. "I'm fine."

He opened the door and gave her a sympathetic expression before pulling her into his embrace like she was little again.

She didn't resist.

And she actually started to feel a little better, allowing her dad to hold her. It was almost like he could make everything okay with a kiss on her knee or elbow. Almost. Now she was too old to believe in such things.

When he started to pull back, she clung to him, wanting to live in a world where problems were solved easily and magic existed.

He rubbed her back. "It's going to be okay."

"Will it?"

"Yes." He kissed the top of her head. "Do you want to sit?"

"I guess." She shrugged and stepped back.

Dad sat on the bed and patted the spot beside him.

She sat, feeling better than before but still guilt-ridden.

"What has you so freaked out? Was it the doorbell, or Nate's mom specifically?"

Hadley played with a nail. "Everything."

"I understand that, but that's a lot to tackle. What's your bigger stress — the guilt or the worry of being caught?"

Tears threatened again. She tried blinking them back. "Both, but the guilt is probably worse. His mom is going to be crushed when she realizes he's dead."

"She's never going to know for sure."

"That's supposed to help?"

"She'll always have the hope that he's out there somewhere."

Hadley frowned, blinking more furiously. The tears were going to win soon.

"People will have to stop looking at some point."

She looked at him like he was crazy. "Would you ever stop looking for me or Zeke or Luna if we disappeared?"

He hesitated. "Not until my dying breath."

"See?"

"Okay, let's try this. The police and social worker won't have the resources to keep searching forever. Other, more urgent cases will come up. They'll have to focus their attention on those. Nate's case will grow cold and forgotten. Life will move on. It always does."

"Not for his family."

"It will. People have to live their lives. They'll remember him on days like his birthday and Christmas, but they'll also have to go to work to pay the bills. Life will go on for them too, it'll just look a lot different from everyone else. His aunt and parents can't keep looking all day, every day. It just isn't feasible."

"That seems unlikely. It's possible to go to work and still focus on searching."

"Day after day? For months on end? Years? No. People need stability, honey. That's too much uncertainty."

"They're going to keep looking at me like I killed him — because I did. It's never going to stop. Ever."

He put his arm around her. "It will, I promise. And the death will never come back to you. He won't be found. Nothing will be."

"You were arrested last night, and you—"

"That was different. I was set up for something I didn't do. Nobody's ever been able to pin anything on me that I actually did."

"Still, that doesn't change the fact that his family will keep looking as long as they live. Even Wes could start demanding answers from jail. And now that his mom has meeting him on her mind, she isn't going to give up." Hadley rubbed her stomach. "I know I wouldn't."

"How about this example? Think about Duke."

The lump in her throat grew bigger. "Why are you bringing him up now?"

"I'm trying to make a point. Stick with me, okay?"

Sighing, she nodded.

"Since he died, life has moved on. Obviously, you haven't forgotten about him, and you probably never will, but you've had to carry on. Circumstances have demanded it."

Hadley wiped a tear away. "What does that have to do with anything?"

"You still miss him, you're still in mourning, but you can't spend all your time focused on the grief. The same is true for Nate's family. They're going to have to drop the search, focus on other things."

"Seriously? Like what?"

"Work and school. Each other. Health issues. Who knows what else? Life has a way of bringing us things we have no choice but to deal with. Nobody escapes it. Everyone will remember Nate, miss him. But they won't be able to put him front and center forever. That's just the way it is."

Hadley sighed, not yet fully convinced. As much as she hated to admit it, Dad had a point about Duke. Immediately after he'd died, she'd been unable to think of anything else. But as much as his loss still killed her, she was forced to think about other things most of the time.

"Just give it time. Right now, everyone's grasping at straws."

"Except that they're not wrong."

"They don't know that."

She twisted a strand of hair, trying to believe that people would eventually stop looking for Nate. But even if they did, that wouldn't change the fact that she was walking around feeling guilty for what she'd done. "How do you deal with the guilt? Does that go away, too?"

"My first kill was different. I was prepared for it, trained."

"But you still felt guilty, didn't you?"

"Of course."

"So, how do you live with it?"

Dad hesitated slightly. "I focused on how I was doing a service to the world by getting rid of someone who'd done such heinous things."

Hadley's face fell. She stared at a loose thread on her sock. "I can't tell myself anything like that."

"No, but you *can* focus on how scared you were. How Nate left you with no other choice. What else were you supposed to do?"

"Anything other than kill him!"

Dad's expression tightened. "But between Wes's earlier threat and Nate threatening you with that video, anyone else would've done the same."

"I should've gone to the police, though. Not covered it up."

"What's done is done, and now you can carry on with your life as you should." He leaned over and kissed the top of her head again. "And for the time being, that means getting some rest. Why don't you get some sleep?"

"Do you think my guilt will ever go away?"

"Yes, once you accept the fact that you were acting in self-defense. There was no other option, given the situation he and his dad put you in."

"I guess so."

"And I know so." He rose and patted her shoulder. "Get some sleep. You'll feel better in the morning."

"Do you? Feel better the next day, after your, uh, jobs?"

He nodded and gave her a reassuring smile. "I sure do."

Maybe one day she would experience the same thing.

Chapter Ten

BRAD PEEKED AROUND THE CORNER. His mom was already engaged in a card game with two other ladies about her age.

He breathed a sigh of relief. At first, she'd balked at the idea of an adult daycare. He'd worried that dropping her off at the place Agent Bancroft had found would be about as successful as the first day he and Faye had taken Hadley to Montessori preschool — their little prodigy had kicked, screamed, and cried. By the time he and Faye stepped outside the building, he wasn't sure if his daughter or wife had shed more tears.

Thankfully, his mom hadn't been nearly so dramatic. She'd pouted in the car, but cheered up when the center's owner greeted them and told her about all the activities they offered. His mom was eager to try the sushi-making class that afternoon.

If this went well, they might continue with the daycare center even after Faye opened her in-home salon.

But for now, he needed to focus on becoming Kurt's best friend.

That thought sent an icy chill down his back.

He needed to suck it up and start acting, regardless of how he felt. If he found it too hard, he would hit up Hadley for tips. The girl had been the lead in every school play for as long as he could remember. Rarely did she get cast in a supporting role, and never had she gotten stuck with a nonspeaking part. If anyone could help him trick his boss, it was her.

How ironic was it that father and daughter would be giving each other advice on how to get away with morally questionable actions? He was teaching her how to live with murder, and she would be giving him tips on deception.

Brad turned his thoughts to BlueBlade. It felt like it had been forever since he'd set foot in the shop. But he couldn't wait to sees Kurt's face — the shock of discovering that yet another of his attempts to shut Brad up had failed. That alone might make this all worth it.

Brad parked in the employee lot, looking for Kurt's car in back. Hopefully this wouldn't be one of those weeks when he didn't come in. Or maybe that would be better. It'd give him time to prepare. He didn't *feel* ready to convince his boss they were now BFFs.

But he would do it. He did what was necessary. And he would do this.

Or maybe he should try to break into Kurt's office and steal the information Bancroft wanted.

No, if he set off an alarm before he found it, he'd also have blown his shot at getting close to Kurt. And he had to make Bancroft happy in order to get immunity.

Full immunity. His killings *hadn't* been legal.

That thought made his blood boil. All the lies he'd been fed. The same lies they'd given his dad, that had gotten him killed.

Those lies had nearly gotten Brad put away for life.

Kurt was going down. Not only for his dad's murder, but for everything he'd done to Brad.

He squeezed the steering wheel, fire burning in his chest. That was the fuel he needed to deceive his boss.

Brad cut the engine and stepped outside, the cold mist spraying his face.

His boss's car was parked on the other side of one of the dumpsters.

Good.

Brad couldn't wait to start his show.

He turned on the agent's wire, set his car's alarm, and marched toward the back door. Unlocked it and stepped inside.

Quiet. The employee's room was empty, but some stray wrappers on the table evidenced the people who were out front, manning the shop. Light shone from underneath Kurt's office door.

Brad's heart pumped harder. He took a few measured breaths. Stared at the door. Imagined his boss on the other side, plotting deaths that would serve him rather than society. The people he wanted dead weren't murderers and rapists — or if they were, Kurt didn't care. He was only interested in the political wins.

Or possibly only the money. People with more money than the Bergmanns were likely behind this, telling Kurt who they wanted dead and paying obscene amounts of money for the completed job.

Bancroft hadn't explained how this business really worked. She'd only given the bare details. Brad's targets had to do with money and politics. Not making the world a better place. In fact, those deaths had probably made things a whole lot worse for a lot of innocent people.

And Kurt and Ralf were swimming in money because of it.

It was sick and twisted. Brad's only peace came from knowing that he would be helping to take them down. To finally put an end to all of it. Not just the Bergmanns and BlueBlade, but also whoever was behind the car wash.

The whole organization was going down.

Swallowing back a grin, Brad marched toward the office door.

He knocked.

Waited.

Knocked again.

Rustling sounded on the other side.

Then came Kurt's voice. "Jeff? Slide the envelope under the door."

"This isn't Jeff."

"Todd?"

"Not Todd, either." The corners of Brad's mouth twitched. He stifled the movement as soon as it happened.

"Who is it?"

Hurried footsteps sounded before the door flung open.

Kurt's eyes widened as he looked at Brad, the realization slowly registering.

"Surprised to see me?" Brad flashed him a quick smile.

"I, uh, I thought you were——"

"Arrested?"

Kurt tugged at his collar. "Yeah. I'd heard what Faye said, though she was stumbling over her words and not making much sense. Hadn't heard anything from you, so I assumed you were still behind bars."

"I was released due to lack of evidence. Isn't that great news?" Brad grinned even wider.

His boss's eyes dilated, and he cleared his throat. "That's ... it's unexpected news."

"Right?" Brad stepped inside like he owned the place.

"It feels great to be back here. Seems like it's been so long. But you wanted me back, and here I am."

"Here you are."

Brad glanced around the office, taking everything in as quickly as possible, seeing it with new eyes. Before, he'd never paid much attention to anything but Kurt. Now it was imperative that he figure out where his boss might be hiding the information Bancroft needed.

This would take time. Kurt kept the top of his desk clear and tidy, with not a single paper strewn anywhere. No opportunity to walk over and quickly read over something.

Was he arrogant enough to keep everything in the desk or one of the file cabinets? Or would he use a more secure location, like a hidden safe?

Kurt cleared his throat and sat in his chair. "When did you get released?"

Brad sat opposite him and kicked up his feet. Linked his fingers through each other behind his head. "First, Faye couldn't reach my attorney, and you couldn't reach yours. I've got some luck, huh?"

Kurt nodded, his expression pinched.

"But just when I thought all hope was lost, bam, in walked my saving grace." Brad let the silence linger a moment. "I could hardly believe it. She worked some kind of magic, and I became a free man once again. At first, I was assuming that my security clearance had pinged, or that you'd called the higher-ups and asked them to pull some strings."

Kurt looked like he was trying to swallow something nasty. "When my lawyers didn't respond, that was my only other choice. But I hadn't heard anything yet."

"I knew you wouldn't let me down," Brad said. "But it turned out that one of Faye's clients recommended a lawyer. Not as expensive as yours, of course, but available when we needed her."

"That's probably why I never got a call back — you were probably already out by the time the big boss got my message."

Brad leaned forward in his chair. "I'm ready to jump in and tackle new targets. Got anyone for me?"

"You'll have to give me time. I wasn't expecting you to come in this morning."

"I'm sure you weren't. If you don't have anything for me to do, I can help you out in here. Or I can go home for the day and come back tomorrow. I could sure use the rest, and I definitely have some damage control to do in my neighborhood. Any idea what it's like to be arrested in front of your family and friends?"

"Can't say that I have."

"What do you want me to do?"

"Don't you need to talk with your attorney? I'm more than happy to give you all the time you need for that."

Brad shook his head. "The arrest was just a misunder-standing."

"But, eh, wasn't there a weapon with your fingerprints? That's what Faye said."

Brad adjusted his weight in the seat. "And it was so generous of you to offer help. I know the attorney you called didn't actually do anything, but you can't be held responsible for that. I'm sure your people are incredibly busy."

"Like you wouldn't imagine."

"So busy, they ignored your call even though you've paid them a hefty retainer."

"For me and my father. Not for you, unfortunately."

"Even though my arrest endangers both of you?"

"We have measures in place to manage that risk."

"That's what I figured. So, I waited — and you wouldn't believe how slowly time goes by in a tiny holding cell with a paper-thin mattress — knowing that justice always prevails. I can't thank you enough for being there for me in my time of greatest need."

Kurt looked at his hand like it was a snake, but shook it. "You can always count on me. I'll be sure to talk with my attorney to find out what happened."

"Don't bother. Everything worked out." Brad stepped toward the door, once again scanning the room for the most likely places Kurt would hide his most valuable information, wishing he had more time.

"I'm sure I speak for everyone when I say how glad I am to hear about your safe release."

Brad glanced at Kurt's pants, expecting them to go up in flames. "I appreciate it. See you in the morning."

"See you then." Kurt gave him an obviously forced smile.

Brad waved as he left and collapsed into the driver's seat once in his car, nerves shot from acting like he didn't want to break his boss's nose. Sure, it had been somewhat fun toying with him, but if he had his way, he would never look at the man again — not unless it was *him* behind bars.

Hopefully that would be soon enough.

In the meantime, he had things to do.

He texted the agent to let her know he'd spoken with Kurt.

She wanted him to come to her office straight away.

Brad started his car and headed in that direction.

Halfway there, he noticed a car following him.

He took a few quick turns.

The car was still behind him.

Chapter Eleven

BRAD PULLED into a full parking lot at a home goods store and weaved through the lanes, looking back at the gray SUV that hadn't left his rearview in the twenty minutes he'd been trying to lose him. And Brad knew how to deal with these situations.

A white minivan pulled out in front of him. He turned on his blinker and took the spot, still able to see the SUV one row over.

Brad dug his phone out of his jacket and called the agent.

"I thought you'd be here by now," she answered.

"Someone is tailing me."

"Describe the vehicle."

"Gray SUV. A few dents on the front, but otherwise nondescript."

"Okay. Where are you now?"

He told her.

"And you've been trying to lose him since you texted me almost a half hour ago?"

"Most of that time, yes. This guy is good. I'd have lost anyone else by now."

"Okay. Change of plans, then."

Brad drew a deep breath. "What?"

She dropped the name of a French restaurant at one of the nearby lakes. "Meet me there."

"Why there?"

"It'll look like you're there for a romantic meal."

"Excuse me?"

"That'll explain why you've been driving around, making the person think you don't suspect you're being followed — that you were trying to be elusive for other reasons."

Brad sighed.

"We both know who's behind this. Let Kurt think something is going on, that you're having marital troubles. Give him a reason to look at something else other than what's really happening."

"I need to let Faye know the plan before I do anything."

"That's fine. I'll reserve a table before leaving. It'll be under your name. Is that SUV still in view?"

Brad glanced over. It was parked exactly one row behind him. If the windows weren't tinted, he'd be able to see who was after him. "Yes."

"Okay, good. Go inside the store and buy something. Look legit. Then meet me in a half hour."

"I don't need anything."

"You need to look natural. Just get something. I don't care what."

"Fine."

"Half hour." She ended the call.

He squeezed the steering wheel. Glanced over at the SUV. Cursed the driver.

Then got out and marched toward the building. He hated everything about the plan, but it beat the holding cell.

Inside, he found and purchased a fitting for a garden hose. Looked around for anyone who might be watching him. Didn't see anyone.

Once outside, he glanced over at the SUV. Still there. There was enough sun to see the outline of a person in the driver's seat.

His pulse raced, and he resisted the urge to march over and demand answers. Instead, he made a show of putting the paper bag into his trunk before getting in and starting the car again.

The SUV pulled out just as Brad did. Kept its distance, but took the same path.

Brad made several odd turns as he headed for the restaurant, and even though he took some at the last moment, the SUV kept following. That driver would not be deterred.

He came to train tracks, and the lights flashed, indicating a train.

Brad lifted his foot, tempted to test fate. He'd lose the SUV for sure. But it was too close. Wasn't going to risk his life to lose the idiot behind him.

As he waited for the train to pass, he remembered he needed to let Faye know what was going on. If it looked like he was going to have a romantic lunch with the agent, he couldn't leave room for errors.

He texted her: *Mtg the agent 4 lunch. Someone is following me, so I can't go to her office.*

Faye must've been on a break, because she called him right away.

"What do you mean someone's following you?" she asked as soon as he answered.

"I'm sure Kurt sent someone to tail me."

"Are you still being followed?"

"You'd better believe it. I'm sure Kurt isn't taking any more chances. He knows something's up."

"I take it you already spoke with him?"

"Yep." Brad craned his neck, looking for the last car of the train. No caboose in sight. "He was shocked to see me. Said he had no work for me, stumbled over himself to get me out of there. If I didn't hate him so much, it would've been hilarious. I'm sure he's trying to figure out how I got released without his help."

"Yeah, I'll bet. What are you going to do about the person following you?"

"I'm going to let him sit in the restaurant's parking lot while I fill the agent in on everything. But I wanted to let you know what's going on, because it could look suspicious. We aren't meeting in her office is because I'm being tailed."

"I appreciate it, and trust you. I hate that I doubted you with Rose."

Brad sighed. "I can't hold that against you. She was *trying* to elicit that reaction from you."

"Bygones." Faye cleared her throat. "I've got to get to my next client. Let me know when you get to the restaurant. I want to know you got there safely."

"I've dealt with worse."

"I know. But I'd feel better."

"Then I'll text you."

"Thank you."

"Faye, I love you."

"I love you too."

He ended the call and stared at the train that seemed to be attempting a world record for the number of cars it was carrying. The line of vehicles behind him was now beyond what he could see.

And the gray SUV was still two cars back.

Pressure built behind his eyes.

He turned just in time to see the end of the train down the track.

Finally.

It took a minute to pass Brad, and another before the gate went up and the light turned green. Brad raced through the intersection, his pulse on fire.

The car behind him turned at the light.

Now the SUV was directly behind him. Though it was leaving a significant amount of space. Not very subtle, but that was obviously not what the driver was going for.

He wanted Brad to know he was there.

And he'd succeeded in that.

He didn't care about losing the tail. Let him think that Brad was having an affair. It would only serve to distract the Bergmanns from Brad's true intention.

He drove slowly, now purposefully trying to annoy the other driver. Thanks to the train, he was already late meeting the agent. What was a few more minutes?

Once Brad reached the restaurant, he had to drive around the lot a few times before finding a spot. The SUV was still making its rounds as Brad headed into the restaurant.

He didn't need to ask about the reservation, as Bancroft was sitting at a table by a large window, waving at him.

She embraced him longer than necessary when he arrived, and let her hand linger on his as she said hello.

He sat, looking around for anyone he knew. Even though he'd already told Faye about the lunch, the agent was giving the impression that they were there for more than business.

Thankfully, he didn't recognize anyone.

"Did you ever lose that car?" she asked.

He picked up the menu. "Nope. It's in the parking lot."

"Good."

Brad raised a brow.

"Point it out to me when we leave, assuming it's still there."

"What good will that do?"

"I'll take care of the driver."

"Meaning?"

She took a sip from the full wine glass in front of her. "You won't have to worry about him, or her, after today."

"Gotcha."

Bancroft's foot ran down the length of his shin.

He took his own glass and gulped down the alcohol like it was water. "So, uh, Kurt was surprised to see me at work today."

She gave him a sultry smile. "I'm sure he was."

"Yep." He raised the menu to block his view of her.

Her foot wrapped around his.

Faye. He pictured Faye.

Remembered he was supposed to text her when he arrived safely.

He dropped the menu. "I need to text my wife."

"Go right ahead." She batted her lashes and moved her foot underneath the cuff of his pants.

Brad leaned over the table. "What are you *doing*?"

"Putting on a show." She nodded toward the left. "See that guy with the goatee?"

Brad glanced in the direction. A guy with a salt-and-pepper goatee sat by himself a few tables over.

"He's at a romantic restaurant alone, and he stepped out of a gray SUV."

Brad's stomach knotted. "Really?"

She leaned forward, close enough that she could brush his lips with hers. Thankfully, she didn't. "Yes. And think of all the juicy details he's going to share with Kurt. It's going to send him in all the wrong directions."

"As long as I don't end up back in jail."

He waited for her to assure him he wouldn't.

She didn't.

"I'm not going back, right? That's the deal."

"If you get framed again, I'll get you out. It's no big deal."

"No big deal?"

"Yeah." She glanced toward the goatee before grabbing Brad's shirt and forcing her mouth on his.

He pulled back, but she had too tight a grip.

"Don't fight it." She pulled back.

"I'm a happily married man."

"One who's lucky to be walking free."

"Doesn't change the fact that I'm *married*."

She leaned closer. "Or the fact that you've killed dozens of people — illegally."

He gritted his teeth.

"Just something to keep in mind."

Brad leaned back as far as possible. "I'm well aware of the facts."

"And you know what I need from you. What your country needs from you."

"Now I'm supposed to be the all-American hero?"

"Something like that."

The waiter came and took their orders.

Brad ordered something small, finding that his appetite had all but disappeared.

Once they were alone again, Bancroft leaned forward. "What's your plan? This needs to happen quickly."

"If it's too fast, mistakes will happen."

"You won't let that happen." Her foot rested on his.

"No. But I also won't gain his trust in a day. Some things do take time."

"Then do what you can in the meantime. Dig like you never have before. You're already quite proficient. Become an expert."

His skin bristled. "I already am."

"There's always room for improvement." She glanced to the side. "Oh, good. Our appetizers are here."

"Wonderful," he mumbled.

Brad picked at the food, barely paying attention to it as the agent continued her foot action and alluring glances.

"Who are you trying to put on a show for?" he asked.

"Anyone who may be watching with intent."

He glanced around. "Pretty sure we're safe."

"We already know of one person." She flicked her gaze toward the goatee.

Brad sighed.

"How many days do you think it'll take to regain Bergmann's trust? You're one of his top guys, so obviously you had his confidence. It's just a matter of proving yourself trustworthy again."

"It won't happen in an afternoon, like you seem to want."

"I don't think you're going to perform miracles. Just looking for some quick action. These people need to be taken down fast."

"He's already going to be watching me like a hawk, trying to figure out how I got out of that holding cell."

"You'll be fine. Leave it to me to take care of goatee, if he's still hanging around when we're done. Then you can head home and figure out your action plan. Tomorrow, I want a progress report."

"But—"

"Not his head on a platter. I said progress. You can do that much in one day, can't you?"

"Of course."

"Good. Then we shouldn't have any problems."

Brad started to say something, but their meals arrived.

Thankfully, Bancroft didn't talk, and she managed to keep her feet to herself through the meal. That made it all the easier for him to focus on his food.

By the time they gathered their things, goatee was still seated at his table.

"What are you going to do about him?" Brad nodded his way.

"Don't you worry about that. Your only concern is worming your way into the hearts of our two guys. And if you can't do that, you still need to find a way to get the information I need. You can just as easily end up back where we first met."

He clenched his jaw.

She smiled at him. "I look forward to our conversation tomorrow."

The agent marched over to goatee's table and said something.

His expression immediately lit up, and he motioned for her to join him.

She did.

Brad hurried to his car.

He had a lot to do, and not much time to figure out how to do it.

Chapter Twelve

DAD HAD BEEN WRONG — getting sleep *didn't* make Hadley feel better. Accusatory dreams had plagued her until the alarm finally went off. She was a wreck, and nauseated, too. But she wasn't sure if that was from nerves or the pregnancy. Maybe both.

To make matters worse, her classes were taking forever. Dragging on like never before. It felt like everyone was staring at her. Blaming her for Nate's death.

But that was crazy. Nobody knew where Nate was. Most of the talk was about him being *missing*. Most called him a runaway. A few thought he'd been abducted by aliens, but they were idiots. Some did whisper about his potential demise, but most everyone agreed it was understandable that he wanted to get away from everything.

She had to admit it did make sense. Nate's mom was killed by his dad, who was now in jail for the crime. To make matters worse, his aunt was moving the kids away months before Nate could graduate with his class.

Not that he could walk with them now. Thanks to Hadley.

Tears stung her eyes. Pressure squeezed her chest.

She struggled to breathe. To think straight. To focus on what the teacher was saying.

Would any of this get easier when people stopped whispering about Nate? When that social worker stopped following her around school?

At least the day was almost over. As soon as the bell rang, she would be free. With any luck, she could get home without anyone accosting her.

She glanced out the window and saw the social worker looking in.

Hadley needed to ask her dad about that — if the woman was allowed to follow her like this. No, she couldn't question her without an attorney there, but what about this? Wouldn't that be considered harassment? Except they couldn't go to the police or try to get a restraining order, because the police were going to ask a lot of questions. And what if the social worker convinced them to look into Hadley?

The bell finally rang. She raced to her locker, careful to avoid friends and nosy social workers alike. Just as she slammed her locker shut, she realized it was time for the play rehearsal.

That was the last thing she cared about. Nothing that used to be important was even on her radar anymore. Lead role in the play? Who cared? Popularity? Nope.

Hadley wanted to get her diploma and move on with her life. Preferably away from Pine Harbor and all the horrible memories surrounding Duke and Nate.

The only good thing about all the mess with Nate was that it took her mind off the grief of Duke's death.

Hadley turned around and nearly crashed into the social worker. "Do you mind?"

STACY CLAFLIN & NOLON KING

"I thought we couldn't talk without your lawyer present."

Hadley glared at the woman before darting around her and heading for rehearsal.

It was time to quit. Not that anyone would care. Several others would be thrilled — they'd get the chance to snatch her role. Let them have it. She had too much to deal with anyway. Not to mention how much harder it would be to give her best performance. Regardless of what happened with Nate's investigation, it wouldn't change anything. Not even if everyone suddenly forgot about him. She would know the truth. That she'd killed him. Nothing could undo that.

Someone tapped her shoulder.

Hadley's heart skipped a beat, and the sound of blood rushed in her ears. Stomach twisted.

Holding her breath and gritting her teeth, she whipped around.

Lucy held up her hands. "Whoa. Everything okay?"

Hadley released her breath. "I'm a little on edge."

"Want to talk about it?"

Her heart sank. If only she could talk — but everything was off limits.

"Ellie's pretty mad, huh?"

With everything else going on, Hadley had nearly forgotten about her best friend hating her. Not that she could blame her, at least not if she was honest with herself. Before the days when Hadley had so much to hide, they told each other everything. Now she couldn't talk to Ellie about anything.

"You poor thing." Lucy wrapped her arms around Hadley. "Let's find somewhere to talk."

"We have rehearsal."

"Not today."

"We don't?"

Lucy shook her head, getting hair in Hadley's face. "We're supposed to practice the dance scene in groups today. You don't remember?"

Hadley sighed. That didn't even sound familiar, and she was sure she'd been at the last rehearsal. Or had she?

"Where do you want to go?" Lucy asked. "You'll have to drive, because my car's in the shop."

Everything felt like it was spinning around her — out of control, like her life.

"The chocolate shop?" Lucy suggested, stepping back. "I don't know about you, but caramel and chocolate sound perfect right about now."

Hadley wasn't even sure she'd be able to taste the sweets.

"I might even have a coupon." Lucy dug into her bag. "They almost never give discounts, but last time I was there, I put in a big order for Dane's birthday." She dug around some more. "I think this is — it is! Bogo. Score!"

Hadley just stared, trying to keep up with her friend.

Lucy grabbed her arm. "Come on. My treat."

Before she knew it, Hadley was starting her car.

Lucy was talking a mile a minute. Something to do with some guys from the wrestling team and a lost dog.

"You just missed the turn," Lucy said. "Just take the next one. We'll have to go through the gas station parking lot."

Hadley barely made the next turn, and had to weave around a line of cars to get to the specialty chocolate shop. Her chest tightened, but she did think of one positive — the social worker was nowhere in sight.

Her friend continued with her story of the lost pup and the wrestlers as they made their way inside the building.

The mouth-watering aromas pulled Hadley from her guilt-laden thoughts.

Lucy turned to her. "Does caramel sound good?"

Hadley nodded.

"Great." Lucy smiled. "Why don't you grab us a table, and I'll get the chocolates?"

"I can go in halves."

"Seriously, girl. It's my treat. Just find us seats."

"If you're sure."

Lucy nudged her toward the tables by the shelves full of games and books.

Hadley stumbled and made her way over, picking an overstuffed couch with a coffee table in front of it filled with picture books from around the world. She picked up one from London. A city she and Duke had dreamed about visiting. Same as they had so many vacations together — backpacking through Europe, lounging on the beaches of Hawaii, cruising to Alaska, and so much more.

None of that would ever happen now.

Tears misted her eyes as she flipped through the pages of the book, imagining herself hand-in-hand with Duke in front of the famous buildings.

Had Nate ever wanted to go there?

The lump in her throat nearly choked her.

She had to stop herself from leaping up and running to her car to spend the rest of the day under her covers. She couldn't leave Lucy high and dry.

Hadley glanced over at her friend, wondering what was taking her so long.

Lucy was still at the counter, deep in conversation with the girl piling little chocolates into a box.

Hadley allowed a few tears to fall, and quickly wiped them away.

If only she could go back in time. First, she'd find a

way to prevent Duke's murder. Then she'd stop herself from killing Nate. But maybe if Duke had never died, she'd have never killed Nate.

She would've been so wrapped up in her secret relationship that she wouldn't have had time to start a friendship-gone-wrong with Nate. She'd have been next door with Duke the night Mom made her go to the movies with Zeke when they'd run into Nate.

It was all a horrific string of events.

The only thing that wouldn't be different would be Ellie's anger at her for hiding her relationship with Duke.

Lucy sat down next to Hadley, handing her a white paper cup and a box of chocolates.

"You bought all of this?"

She nodded, sipping her drink.

"I can't let you pay for everything."

"You didn't. I only paid for mine. Yours was free."

"That's not what I mean."

Lucy opened her box of chocolate. "Stop being such a worrywart. I want to use my coupon on you. Now drink that mocha before it gets cold."

It was hot in her hand, even with the thick paper, so it was doubtful that it would cool anytime soon, but she sipped it, anyway. It wasn't just a mocha — it was a sugary-sweet white chocolate mocha.

"You don't have to talk if you don't want to. I know you have a lot on your plate, between all the stuff with your dad and Ellie being mad at you. Plus, I can't even imagine what you're going through after what happened to Duke. I'd be falling apart with just any of those things." Lucy leaned back and popped a candy into her mouth. "I don't know how you're holding yourself together so well."

Hadley cleared her throat. "It isn't easy."

"At least chocolate can help make it better for a few minutes."

They sat in silence for a little while, sipping the coffees and eating too many chocolates. It would take hours of exercise to burn off all the calories, but Hadley didn't care. And there was no reason to. Not when she was going to be gigantic soon, anyway.

Her phone buzzed with a text.

Ellie.

Hadley's heart raced. Was she ready to hear her out?

Ellie: U won't talk to me but u will w/Lucy?! WTH?

Hadley sat up and looked around. Couldn't see her best friend. Or anyone from school who would've told her where Hadley was.

Hadley: She invited me to hang out.

Ellie: Whatever.

Hadley: She needed a ride home. Wanted to stop here.

Ellie: Whatever.

Hadley: I tried talking to u at lunch but u walked away.

Ellie: Whatever.

Hadley: I'm done w/this. If u actually want to talk, LMK.

Ellie: Whatever.

Hadley's blood boiled.

Lucy arched an eyebrow. "Everything okay?"

"Yeah." Hadley shoved her phone in her bag where it belonged. "I'm ready to talk, if you're ready to listen."

"Girl, you know I am."

Hadley drew a deep breath and considered where to start. She definitely wasn't going to talk about killing Nate, but she could talk about how much losing Duke sucked and how crappy it felt to have her best friend not understand.

Maybe she'd even open up about the pregnancy.

Maybe.

Chapter Thirteen

BRAD'S NECK and shoulders ached from hunching over the laptop as he typed furiously. He'd get a heating pad later. For now, he had to focus. The rabbit trail he'd found on the dark web was leading closer and closer to the Bergmanns. There were enough references to the Slippery Fish and RB — Ralf Bergmann — that Brad knew he was getting close.

No, he wasn't inside the enormous Bergmann home staring at an open file cabinet, but this was as close as he was going to get without having to convince Kurt that they were buddies.

Just the thought of having to suck up to him like that was enough to make Brad want to take a hot shower and scrub his skin raw.

He was grateful for the internet. It must've been so much harder doing his job in the days before the web was ubiquitous. The thought of trying to find anything in the days of dial-up made his skin crawl.

Brad continued clicking around, hunching closer to the screen. Ignoring the pains in his neck and shoulders.

Found a link to Kurt's name. No code or abbreviations. His actual name.

Brad's pulse raced.

He moved the curser to the link.

Clicked it.

Watched as the screen started to load the new site.

Something beeped.

Everything turned black.

His stomach dropped.

A link couldn't do that.

Could it?

He sat up straight and looked around. Couldn't see anything in the pitch-black room. There wasn't even any light coming from underneath his office door.

Beep.

The internet box. That meant the power was out. If he hadn't been so focused on the website, he'd have figured that out straight away.

He rose and stretched his neck. Crept to the window, careful not to trip over anything. He'd been throwing paper and files carelessly as he'd hunted through his father's files for more information.

Lifting his blinds revealed a dark street. Nobody had power.

At least it wasn't just his house. It wouldn't have surprised him if it was, given how much time he'd spent on the dark web. His activity was supposed to be untraceable, but nothing was foolproof.

Nothing.

A good-sized branch flew through the air. Some leaves brushed against the window. Rain pelted the glass.

He'd better get downstairs and check on his family. Someone might need his help. The last thing he needed was for his mom to fall and injure herself *again*. With everything dark, the chances of her doing so rose exponentially.

Brad closed his laptop, grabbed a flashlight, and went into the hall, locking his door behind him. Not like it mattered much anymore. Hadley and Zeke knew about him being an assassin.

At least they didn't know he'd been acting illegally all these years. He'd convinced them that he was one of the good guys, that he was making the world a safer place.

That was what he'd thought.

How wrong he'd been. Now look at where he was. Checking the dark web for dirt on his bosses and their company.

Brad looked in each of the bedrooms, not finding anyone. He headed downstairs, where everyone was gathered in the living room.

Luna was shining a flashlight on the walls, telling people to guess what she was 'drawing.' Hadley was pacing and muttering to herself behind the couch.

Brad put his arm around her. "Are you okay?"

"Not even close."

Everyone else appeared fine, so he led his oldest to the kitchen. "What's wrong?"

She collapsed onto one of the chairs. "Everything!"

"Can you be more specific? Give me something I can help with."

"You can't fix anything."

"Are you sure about that?" He sat next to her and set the flashlight on the table so that the beam shined on the ceiling. "I can't do *anything*?"

"No."

A crack of thunder shook the walls.

Hadley screamed.

Brad scooted his chair closer. "You're never this jumpy. What's going on?"

"What if someone is trying to get in?"

"The house?"

"No. The Space Needle." She rolled her eyes.

"Do you want my help or not?"

"I didn't *ask* for your help. You're the one who brought me in here."

He silently counted to ten and reminded himself that she was hormonal and probably on edge from the storm and the power outage. "You seem more upset than usual."

"How upset am I usually?" She scowled.

He counted again. "Nothing like this."

"I don't want to talk about it. There's nothing you can do."

"You don't know that until you let me in."

"Yes, I do. Trust me."

Annoyance ran through him. "Okay, I'll leave, then. If you decide you want to talk to me, I'll be in the living room."

She didn't say anything.

He stood.

"Wait."

"You think I'm actually useful?"

Hadley's gaze darted back and forth. "Can you look around outside?"

"What's out there?"

She picked at a nail. "Someone could be in our yard."

"What kind of idiot would be wandering around with branches flying all over the place?"

"The kind that wants me dead."

He tilted his head.

"Everyone is looking at me like I did something to Nate! That stupid social worker—"

"Is she harassing you again?"

"No, but she's been following me at school."

"That would be harassing." He sat back down. "Is she threatening you? Are you carrying a knife again?"

"No! I don't think I'll ever touch another weapon as long as I live."

"You might want to rethink that."

"Will you look outside or not?"

"Are you saying you want me to get hit by a branch?"

"Da-ad. That's not funny."

He shrugged. "You'd really feel better if I have a look?"

"Yes."

"Then I'll look around."

Zeke came in. "Where?"

"Hadley wants me to check outside."

"Why? So a tree can fall on you?"

Brad gave his daughter a knowing look.

"No," Hadley snapped. "Someone could be outside."

"Nobody would be that dumb." Zeke headed for the fridge.

"Don't open that," Brad said. "We have to keep the cold air in until the power comes back on."

Zeke groaned. "We seriously need a generator."

"Well, we don't have one. So find something to eat in the pantry."

A branch hit the window.

Hadley screamed again. "Dad, will you please look outside? That could be a murderer out there."

Zeke looked at her like she was crazy. "You really think a killer is out there throwing branches at our window in the middle of a storm?"

"It's not impossible."

He pulled out a box of granola bars. "Seriously? Think about it — there are two killers living in the house. Anyone would be stupid to break in here. *They* would be the ones to get offed."

"I'm not a killer!" she exclaimed. "It was an accident."

"Poh-tay-toh, poh-tah-toh."

Hadley turned to Brad. "Would you do something about your son?"

He looked at Zeke. "You need to stop talking about this. Don't bring up either what your sister did or my profession. Not even here in the house. Your grandma and Luna have no idea about any of that, and I'd like to keep it that way."

"Fine." He left the room without the snack box.

Hadley stared at him.

"What? I got him off your back."

"Are you going to look outside?"

"I'll start by looking out the windows."

Thud!

She jumped. "What was that?"

"A branch hit the house."

"Or a killer did!"

"Maybe a branch hit the murderer."

Hadley narrowed her eyes. "Don't make fun of me."

"Why are you so worried that someone is after us?"

"Are you joking?"

"No."

"Because of what I did."

"Nobody even *knows* about that."

"You do. Mom does. Zeke."

"And that's as far as it goes."

"He bled all over me!"

"And those clothes have been properly disposed of. No evidence. And that's what counts."

Thud!

Hadley shuddered. "Won't you just look? I can't take the stress!"

Exhaustion pressed on him. He rose anyway. "If it'll make you feel better, I'll look around."

"Thank you!" She threw her arms around him.

"Just know that I'm going to blame you if a branch hits me in the head."

"Dad."

"I'm serious."

"You'll be fine."

Thud!

"I hope that isn't an omen."

She shook her head. "It's not."

He grabbed a plastic bag to wrap around the flashlight and protect it from the elements. Then he found his raincoat and headed for the back door.

Two more branches hit the house during that time. He considered wearing his old biking helmet.

Unable to find it, he zipped up the jacket as far as the thing would go and made his way to the backyard. Raindrops pelted his face and leaves clung to his jacket. A branch flew past, missing him by a foot.

His breath hitched. There was no way anyone would be out in this mess. Only he lacked the sense to stay indoors, and even that wasn't guaranteed safety. A branch could easily go through a window.

He battled the wind to stand up straight and had to hold his free arm up to block the rain from assaulting his eyes. The flashlight which had been effective inside was faint in the storm, barely illuminating the yard as he crept along the side of the house.

No killers here.

Turned the corner. Still empty. One of the trees near the house scraped against the window with force, so much so that it was likely to leave a scratch if it kept that up. He made his way over and tried to snap the branch.

Too thick.

He held the flashlight between his arm and side, then used both hands to bend the branch. It moved, but didn't break. He tried a different angle.

No difference.

A large soggy leaf smacked him in the face. Stuck to the side of his head.

He swiped at it, dropping the flashlight in the process. After removing the foliage, he bent over and reached for the light.

Stopped cold.

His breath hitched as he stared at what the beam illuminated.

He'd almost stepped on it.

A knife lay tucked under a thick bush, protected from the elements. The dirt underneath was dry, despite the weather.

And that was what allowed him to see the dried blood crusted onto the blade.

Heart thundering, he crouched lower. Moved the flashlight for a better look.

Most of the short blade was crusted with the blood.

What on earth was it doing there? Who had dropped it — or worse, left it intentionally? And more importantly, whose blood was on it?

His mouth dried as he reached for it. He stopped and looked around for something to grab it with.

The bag on the flashlight. His prints would be all over the outside, but the inside would be clean. He hadn't touched that.

Pressing himself against the house protected him from some of the rain, thanks to the eaves. He pulled off the plastic as carefully as possible, avoiding the inside of the bag. Then he knelt. Considered the best way to pick it up.

Managed to get it in the bag without touching any part of the knife. Zipped it closed and released a slow breath.

Now to get it inside without letting anyone see it. Hadley would ask if he found anything. No, she'd ask if he found *anyone*.

If he could get the knife to Agent Bancroft, she could have it analyzed. But he had to do that without alerting his family.

They had enough to worry about without adding this to their plates.

He tucked the knife into an inside pocket in his coat. Not exactly ideal, but he wasn't a cop and he sure wasn't going to call them.

They all thought he was guilty of murder — and for all he knew, this knife was more planted evidence against him. He'd bet on it. Probably linked to the blade that had landed him under arrest.

If there had been an actual bloody knife in that case. He'd never seen anything, and the police were suspiciously tight-lipped about the whole thing.

Brad made his way through the rest of the yard, this time not so sure he wouldn't run into anyone.

It was clear.

Now he needed to contact the agent.

Chapter Fourteen

Brad hurried out of his car as soon as he saw the headlights turn into the parking lot. That could only be Agent Bancroft. Nobody else would be out in this storm. The wind was blowing all kinds of things around and half the traffic lights were out of service.

If he hadn't found a bloody knife on his property, he wouldn't be out in it, either. But given everything else going on, it needed to be dealt with *now*.

He got to the building's door at the same time Bancroft did.

She unlocked it and let them in.

"Thanks for meeting me."

"It sounds like an emergency. Let's get up to the office so I can see it."

He noted that she didn't say *her* office. This was likely something temporary, just for this job. She probably had a cushy office somewhere far more glamorous than Pine Harbor.

Once inside the office, she locked the door behind them. "You just found it tonight?"

"Yeah." He pulled the plastic bag out of his jacket and set it on the table. "My daughter was worried someone was outside, so I was looking around to put her mind at ease. Instead, I found this."

"How did she feel about that?"

"Are you kidding? I didn't tell anyone other than you and my wife. I didn't want to say anything to her, but she could tell immediately that something was wrong."

Bancroft nodded and moved closer to the table, looking at the knife. "Is this one of your company's knives?"

"No. They're called BlueBlade for a reason. Ours are all cobalt blue. And the logo is also at the end of the handle. This looks like your run-of-the-mill department store brand."

She pursed her lips and inched closer, studying it. "You found it in the storm, and it still has all the blood on it?"

"Like I said on the phone, it was under a bush. As you can see from the dirt that got transferred to the bag, it's dry. I found it partially under the house eaves."

"Makes sense."

"Do you have someplace you can take it to be analyzed?"

"Right now?"

"There has to be a lab open for emergencies. Crimes are committed around the clock. Police surely send evidence in at all hours."

"I'm not police."

"I know that, but you have access to everything they do. Don't you?"

She stepped back from the table. "It isn't quite that simple, but I know someone who can take a look at it for me."

Brad paced. "Why would someone put that there? Is it

a message? Or are they trying to frame me for yet another murder?"

"If they are, I'll get you out again. No big deal."

"*Again*? 'No big deal.' Do you know what it's like to be arrested in front of your kids and mother? Your wife? Neighbors?"

"I can't say that I do, but we *are* up against some powerful criminals." She pulled out her tablet. "Tell me everything you know about this knife, starting with how you found it."

He relayed the story as she took notes.

"Anything else?"

Brad tried to remember anything he might've forgotten. "No, that's it."

"Good. I'll get this to my guy. With any luck, we'll have answers by tomorrow."

"Luck? It isn't guaranteed?"

"I'm not the analyst, and I don't know what the testing will involve any more than you do." She slid on gloves and put the knife into another bag before sliding it into her purse. "Go home and get some sleep. You'll need your rest — you have a lot of work tomorrow, convincing the Bergmanns that you're their new best friend."

"It's going to take more time than that."

Her brows drew together. "Time? You want time?"

"It isn't a matter of preference! They aren't going to trust me easily."

"Like I said, you have your work cut out for you tomorrow. Today was the warm-up and tomorrow is the real deal."

"I can't work that quickly."

"And yet you want everything from me right away?" She tilted her head. "I got you out of jail, took care of your arrest record, and met you here in the middle of a storm. You need to pull your weight."

"I *am*. But building trust takes time."

"And the Bergmanns have known you for over a decade, am I correct?"

"Yes."

"Then you have plenty of history to work from. They've had you to their home recently. There's exactly no reason you can't get back into their good graces tomorrow."

His stomach knotted. "No reason? What about the fact that they set me up for murder?"

She stepped closer, leaving little space between them. "You've earned their trust before, get it back. Kiss up as much as you need to. Make promises. I don't care what it takes. We aren't playing around here. If you lose motivation, think back to the holding cell. We both know how you feel about that place."

Brad squeezed his fists. "To make sure we're both on the same page, *exactly* what is expected of me tomorrow? Do you think I'll be able to get into secret files soon? Or get Kurt to spill his guts to me?"

"Ideally."

His mouth fell open. "Seriously?"

"I said that would be ideal. Earn their trust. Provide me with some proof of that. Then we'll work on finding the evidence I need to take down the organization."

"What kind of proof do you need?"

"Your word that they've promoted you, for example. Or an invitation to their home. Something like that. We won't know what the evidence will be until they offer it."

"And this is exchange for a quick turnaround on the knife?"

"Correct. That, and keeping your record clear. I took care of a few outstanding parking tickets, as well."

He forced a smile. More for her to hold over his head. "Great."

"Like I said, go home and get some rest. You're going to need it. Tomorrow's a big day."

"Yes, it is."

They headed to the parking lot in silence. Brad's mind raced. If he came off as too eager, Kurt would smell the insincerity like a fly sniffing out garbage. He could then either fire or kill Brad. And if Brad didn't get on his good side, then Bancroft could undo his immunity. He'd be right back in that holding cell, awaiting prison.

He would be walking a tightrope. Worse: he'd be balancing on a hair, trying to walk between two buildings over a pile of nails set on fire.

And now he had to go home and act like everything was normal. At least Faye knew what was going on. He could talk with her about it. She might even have some ideas on how to get on Kurt's good side. She had a knack for reading people. Brad could charm and deceive, but the Bergmanns were masters at the art. Pulling the wool over their eyes would take a special level of talent.

Something he wasn't sure he had. But he would need to figure that out, or off to prison he'd go.

When he got home, the house was quiet. His mom was sleeping in her makeshift room downstairs.

He used a small flashlight from his keychain to light the way upstairs. The silence was eerie without power to the house. The lack of all the noises he never noticed nearly made his ears ring.

Brad knocked on Zeke's door.

"Who is it?"

"Me." Brad opened the door.

Zeke sat on the floor with Wynn.

Brad turned to his son. "What's he doing here? It's a school night."

"He came here because his stepmom was freaking out."

Wynn shoved him. "She's not my stepmom. Just my dad's girlfriend." He turned to Brad. "She's annoying enough in the light, but a hundred times worse without power."

"Does your dad know you're here?"

"Yeah."

"Okay." Brad reached for the door.

"You don't work when there's no power?" Wynn asked. "Or did you just come back from a kill?"

Brad's stomach churned acid at the reminder of his son's friend knowing his life-or-death secret. Now it was even worse since Brad had discovered that he was not, in fact, a legal assassin. He cleared his throat. "We don't discuss that, remember?"

Wynn looked around. "Nobody else can hear. It's just us."

"Doesn't matter. Remember what we talked about?" Brad narrowed his eyes.

The kid gulped. "Sorry. Yes."

"Good. Don't breathe a word of it to anyone, ever."

Wynn nodded. "Got it."

"Now get some sleep, you two. The power will likely be back on in the morning, and that means school." Brad closed the door behind him and checked on Hadley, who was, thankfully, sleeping. And Luna was snuggled up against her.

It warmed his heart to see his kids taking care of each other.

Faye was in bed, looking at her phone. She glanced up when he walked in. "How'd everything go?"

"She said she'd get it analyzed as soon as possible." He pulled off his shirt.

Faye climbed out of bed. "Did she think someone was setting you up again? Or that someone was sending a message?"

"The agent isn't going to speculate. She just wants to see the results."

"I'm just glad you're home." Faye wrapped her arms around him.

He held her close. "So am I."

She clung to him for a few moments before returning to bed, and he put on an oversized shirt and joined her.

Faye didn't ask any more questions — to his relief. He didn't want to think about, much less talk about, what levels he would have to sink to in order to curry favor with Kurt.

Especially when all he wanted was to take the man's life for murdering his father.

Chapter Fifteen

HADLEY TURNED OFF HER ALARM. Luna wasn't in bed anymore. She must've already gotten up for breakfast. Or maybe she went to her room in the middle of the night.

Not that it mattered. Hadley needed to find out if there was school today.

After yesterday, she would gladly take a day off. Ellie was still not speaking to her, which was fine. If she wanted to be pissy because Hadley was hanging out with Lucy, let her.

Ellie obviously wasn't the friend she'd always pretended to be. If she cared more about the fact that Hadley never told her about Duke than she cared about Hadley's heart-crushing grief over his death, then Hadley was better off without her. In fact, maybe she never told Ellie because deep down she knew her friend wasn't what she pretended to be.

They were, after all, actors. Always getting the good roles.

Maybe that was the only reason they were friends in the first place. Ellie might have only wanted the status.

How could she have not seen that sooner?

It made her wish she'd actually told Lucy about her pregnancy. To give Ellie something to really be upset about. But Hadley had chickened out. It was still her secret to bear.

Hadley shoved Ellie from her mind and checked her phone for updates on school closures as she got up. The switch didn't turn on the light, so that was a good sign.

On social media, all the kids were celebrating the day off.

Just to be sure, she checked the school's website.

The district was closed for the day.

She got back into bed and snuggled under the covers, taking in the good news. An extra day to get her homework done and an excuse to avoid Ellie. She wouldn't have to deal with anybody questioning her about Nate or teasing her about Duke.

Jerks. What kind of people ridiculed someone whose boyfriend had been murdered?

She couldn't wait to graduate and get out of this tiny town full of small-minded people.

Hadley started to close out the social media app when a news article appeared in her feed. Nate's name was in the headline, next to a photo of a charred car.

One that looked like it could be Nate's.

The phone fell from her grasp and bounced on the mattress. She grabbed it and clicked the link. Skimmed it, her pulse drumming in her ears.

It was as bad as it looked.

The burned car was found deep in the forest by a lost hiker who'd gotten stuck in the storm. He'd stumbled upon the destroyed car, partially covered by debris. The hiker had stayed in it all night, claiming that it had saved his life by providing protection from the elements.

According to the article, all of the identifying information had been removed from the car, but they were certain it was the same make and model as the missing teen's. Someone had gone to great lengths to cover it up and hide the identity.

Her stomach lurched. She dropped the phone and ran to the bathroom, just in time to throw up in the toilet.

Dad had promised that nobody would ever find the car.

Now the whole world knew about it. Or they would soon. And they'd realize that Nate hadn't run away — he'd been murdered.

Her entire body trembled. She leaned against the wall for support. Slid down to the floor. The tiny room seemed to shrink, closing in on her.

If Dad was wrong about this, what else was he wrong about? Would someone find Nate's body? What about the blood residue in the park? Or her clothes that he had bled all over? There was also the knife. Dad had taken care of all of that.

Just like he'd taken care of the car.

How long would it be until she was found out? Put in jail for the rest of her life? Sure, it was an accident. Nate was antagonizing her. But she'd lied.

Nobody would see her as innocent now. There wouldn't be any mercy for her. She blew her chance for that when she decided not to confess right away.

Tears blurred her vision. She let them flow freely. What was she supposed to do now? Continue with the lies and hope that Dad was right about her not being caught? He'd promised that no one would ever find that car.

Somebody had. And people were already saying it looked like Nate's.

Because it was.

Hadley shook as she reached for toilet paper and blew her nose.

Knock, knock!

"You done in there yet?" Zeke called.

"There's no school today. Go away!"

"I have to pee. Let me in!" He pounded some more.

"We have other bathrooms."

"Let me in. You don't have to spend hours on makeup today."

She sighed deeply, rose, and looked in the mirror. A mess stared back at her. Red nose, splotchy, puffy skin around the eyes, and hair sticking out in every direction.

"Give me a minute!" She ran her hands through her hair and pulled it up into a messy bun. It wasn't much better, but maybe it was enough for her clueless brother not to notice how she looked.

He gave her a double-take as soon as she stepped out. "What's wrong?"

So much for that.

"Bathroom's yours," she said with a careless wave.

"But what's wrong?"

"Why do you care?" she countered.

"Because we're in on each other's secrets."

"Yeah? Who'd *you* kill?"

He stiffened. "Nobody. You know that. But we're in this together. What's wrong?"

More tears threatened. She cleared her throat. "Check social media."

Then she raced to her room, locking the door.

At least she didn't have to deal with school. People would be all over her, wanting to know about the car. She wouldn't be able to escape it.

Maybe homeschool or virtual school really was the

answer. She could probably even get a doctor's note because of the pregnancy.

Hadley climbed back into bed and pulled the covers over her head. Thought about checking online for updates. Decided against it.

Her warm bed was the perfect place to stay all day.

Knock, knock, knock, knock!

She groaned.

The noise continued.

"Open up!" Zeke called.

"Go away!"

"Do Mom and Dad know?"

"Leave me alone!"

"You do realize these locks are super easy to open, don't you? All I need is a screwdriver. A wire might even work."

She forced herself out of bed, muttering, and opened the door. "Happy?"

He stepped inside. "*Is* it Nate's?"

"Who else's would it be?" She glanced at his shirt. "Go back to your room and listen to Duran Duran."

Zeke closed the door and sat on her bed. "There's no chance it's anyone else's?"

"You'd have to ask Dad."

"So, you don't know?"

"Like I said, who else could it belong to?"

He frowned. "What are you going to do?"

"Sign up for virtual school."

"Really?"

She shrugged.

"You haven't told Mom and Dad?"

"They'll hear about it eventually."

"You have to tell Dad."

"Why? So he can dig me into a deeper hole? He said

nothing would ever be found. What else is he wrong about?"

"He needs to know! So we can figure out what to do next."

"We?"

"Well, yeah. We're family. We're all in this together."

She sighed. "Yet I'm the only one who would go to jail."

"He would, too."

Her stomach flip-flopped. "And Mom helped him. What's going to happen to you and Luna if we all go to prison?"

"Stay with Grandma."

"Somebody has to take care of her, too." Her throat felt like it was going to close, so she couldn't breathe. "I should turn myself in so the rest of you don't get dragged into this."

"But how would you explain all the cover-up?"

"I'll say I did that, too."

"We need to tell Dad. He's going to find out anyway, and he'll know what to do."

"And he needs to explain himself. He said it would be impossible for the car to be found." She marched toward the door.

"That's what I'm talking about." Zeke caught up with her as she opened it.

Her heart pounded. Would Dad know what to do?

Grandma and Luna were downstairs, eating dry cereal.

"Where's Dad?" Hadley asked.

"Your parents went to work," Grandma said. "Do you want some cereal?"

"To work?" Hadley asked. "Without power?"

"It's been restored on that side of town."

Hadley shivered, all of a sudden realizing how cold it was.

"Do you want breakfast?" Grandma asked.

"It's like camping, but inside." Luna beamed.

Hadley forced a smile. "Yeah, just like that." She turned to Grandma. "I'm not hungry, but thanks. Maybe Zeke wants something."

She hurried upstairs before Grandma could insist that she eat. There was no way she could put anything in her stomach right now.

Not with her entire life falling down around her.

After catching sight of her reflection in her vanity mirror, Hadley decided to take a shower. Maybe if she looked better, she would feel a little better. Not that it would change anything.

She caught sight of Duke's house — his *old* house. Now it belonged to a family with three little kids.

It sucked how life moved on whether she wanted it to or not.

Chapter Sixteen

FAYE GRABBED her things from the counter and headed to the employee lounge for lunch. It had been a busy morning with a few drop-ins squeezing in between appointments. The waiting area had been packed since opening. Many people seemed to want a little electricity more than the trims they came in for.

She warmed her food in the microwave before settling onto the couch and digging in. She checked her phone halfway through. Five missed calls from Hadley.

Five.

Something had to be wrong. Was it a pregnancy complication? Something worse?

She scrambled to return the call.

Hadley answered right away. "Where have you been?"

"You know I can't take calls when I'm with clients." She took a deep breath, trying to calm her nerves.

"That's a stupid rule!"

"I agree, and it won't be in place when I have my own salon. Is there an emergency?"

"Yes!"

"Are you in the hospital? Or is it Grandma?"

"No. Nothing like that." The two-second pause felt like an eternity. "They found the car."

"Who? What car?"

"*The* car, Mom. His."

"You can't mean N—"

"Don't say his name!" Hadley interrupted. "Not around others."

"Okay, but are you sure? Dad said that wouldn't be possible."

"Check the news!"

Faye drew in a deep breath. There had to be some mistake. "I'll do that as soon as I get off the phone. It might not be his. It could be anyone's."

"It isn't!" Hadley sounded near tears.

"Have you spoken with Dad? He would know more than I would."

"Neither one of you have been answering! I'm freaking out, and you're both more concerned about work."

"You know that isn't true."

"Isn't it?"

"It's not. We both have rules to follow." Faye played with a loose string on the couch. "Try not to think about this, and I'll see if I can reach Dad."

"Don't think about this?" Hadley exclaimed. "Do you know what this could mean if they put it all together?"

Her mind raced. "Even if they do think it's his, they won't be able to prove anything. Your dad knows how to —" Faye glanced around at the other stylists in the room and tried to think of the most subtle way to speak. "He knows what he's doing."

"But he said they'd never find it! But now they have, and everyone's talking about it!"

"I'll call you back in a few. Put on a movie or

something."

"Are you kidding?"

"You need the distraction."

"Mom, just call him."

Hadley hung up.

Faye stared at the screen, the pain behind her eyes intensifying. How could Nate's car have been found? That wasn't possible — at least, that was what Brad had claimed.

With shaky hands, she gathered the rest of her lunch and put it in the fridge before heading outside. She had to walk a little way down the sidewalk to get away from others' ears. Considering how cold and windy it still was, there were a lot of people out and about.

She settled on a bench and started to call Brad, but then stopped herself. Before speaking to him, she needed to see the news herself. She couldn't base everything on what Hadley had said. It was possible she was blowing something unrelated completely out of proportion.

Or maybe that was just what Faye hoped.

She opened the local news app on her phone, and sure enough, it was on the main page, right underneath a storm update.

A car was found by a lost hiker who had used it for shelter during the worst of the wind the night before. He'd found it partially covered by tree branches, and though it'd been severely burned, the metal shell had protected him from the elements until he was able to find his way out of the woods.

Most of what was being reported about the car itself was speculation by the authorities and the reporters. It was a sedan that looked like it *could* be the make and model of Nate's missing car. There was nothing of Nate's inside the vehicle and the only prints found were from the hiker.

Relief washed through her. It would be next to impossible to prove it was his — assuming the car actually was Nate's. There was no way to know without Brad's confirmation. He hadn't given any details about his disposal of the car because he didn't want anyone to use it against Hadley or Faye.

It was time to hear his side.

She pulled out her phone. Not much time left, but what was her boss going to do if she made the client wait for a few minutes? Fire her?

Brad's phone went to voicemail, just as Hadley had said.

Faye immediately called again.

And again.

Until he finally answered. "What's going on?"

"Have you checked the news?"

"I'm a little busy. What's the problem?"

"A charred sedan was found in the woods. Do we need to be concerned?"

"Come again?"

"A burned car was buried under branches until the storm removed them and a hiker used it as a place to sleep through the night."

Brad swore.

"So, it's as bad as it sounds?"

"There isn't any way they can link it to the kid. None." Rustling sounded on the other end. "Hold on a minute. I'm going to call you right back."

"But I don't—"

The call ended.

"Have much time." She sighed.

As promised, a minute later he returned the call. "I'm in my car where I won't be overheard."

"Are you *sure* it can't be linked to him?"

STACY CLAFLIN & NOLON KING

"Yes."

"You also said nobody would ever find it."

"I'm not sure that I said *never*. But I couldn't have foreseen this turn of events. The massive windstorm, the lost hiker — it's a terrible coincidence. The debris covering the car should've stayed in place, and grown stronger with time as moss grew to hold it in place. Then it should've slowly destroyed the—"

"Okay, okay. I believe you. But now that we're here, what do we have to worry about?"

"The fire should've destroyed any evidence. Finger-prints, stray hairs, you name it."

"Are you sure?"

"Yes. Also, I removed the VIN number, and the plates are nowhere near the car."

"You took everything out of the glove compartment? The middle console? What about the trunk?"

"Yes, yes, and yes. All taken care of. Like I said, there's nothing there to link it to Nate. Speculation won't hold up in court. And it certainly won't point anyone in our direction."

Faye pinched her nose again. "I hope you're right."

"I am."

"You're not worried at all?"

"More annoyed than anything."

"Annoyed?"

"Yeah. I went to a lot of trouble to make sure nobody would find it. Had to wait for the fire to cool before covering it — and that was a lot of work in and of itself."

Faye tried to piece together how they managed to do everything that night. It all seemed like such a blur. "Did you get any sleep that night?"

"I don't think so."

"What are we going to do?"

114

"Carry on like normal."

"Are you serious?" she exclaimed.

"We don't have any other choice. I'm just glad the kids are at home, and don't have to deal with that social worker. I don't know how she has so much time to follow them around at school."

"Hadley brought up virtual school. Maybe we should consider that."

"If she pulls out, it's going to raise a red flag."

"People are already questioning her. We need to think more about her wellbeing than what others will say."

"Let me think about it," he said. "Have you spoken with her?"

"She's the one who told me about the car. To say she's worried would be an understatement."

"Did you tell her it was under control?"

"I reassured her that you know what you're doing."

"Good. Let me look into it, and I'll get back to you."

Faye glanced at the time. One minute to get ready for her next client. "Okay. If I can't answer right away, I'll call as soon as I can."

"Good. Carry on as normal. That's the best we can all do to keep from raising any suspicions."

"Sure. No problem."

He sighed. "I didn't say this would be easy, but it's manageable. We've got this."

"I hope you're right."

"I am. Just focus on your client. I'll even call Hadley. Looks like she was trying to call me, too."

"I'm sure she'll appreciate hearing directly from you."

They ended the call, and Faye hurried back to the salon.

It would take a miracle to stay focused now.

Chapter Seventeen

BRAD ENDED the call and closed his eyes. It had taken longer than expected to calm his daughter down about the car, but he had finally convinced her that nobody would be able to positively link it to Nate. And even if they did, it would be impossible to find any evidence pointing to Hadley, or to Brad.

He should've taken it deeper into the woods. But it had been risky enough towing Nate's car so that he had a getaway nearby. Everything that night had put them in danger of exposure. He'd had zero time to plan, or think anything through.

It was no wonder something like this had gone wrong. But he'd made the best possible choices, given the circumstances. And it was all to protect his daughter.

He would do it all again in a heartbeat. She'd been under more pressure than he could imagine dealing with at that age — and that was on top of the pregnancy and loss of her boyfriend.

Wes, who had been threatening her, was responsible for

all of this. He'd set it all in motion by killing his wife and framing Brad, then threatening Hadley.

She and Nate were the innocent victims in this whole thing. Brad couldn't help Nate, but he would do everything in his power to get his daughter out of this mess.

His phone buzzed with a text. Probably Faye wanting an update.

It buzzed again before he had a chance to look at it.

Agent Bancroft.

What could she want?

Brad unlocked the phone and checked.

Bancroft: Call me now.

Bancroft: Immediately.

His stomach plunged. What now?

Only one way to find out.

He called her number.

"What do you know about that local missing kid?" she demanded.

"Missing kid?"

That was what she wanted to talk about?

"Yes." Her tone was sharp. "The one all over the news."

"He went missing, and everyone has been looking at my family."

"Did you do it?"

"Do what? Everyone says he's a runaway."

"A runaway whose destroyed vehicle was just discovered. All evidence removed. A job that thorough could only be done by someone who knew what he was doing."

His heart hammered. No way was he having this conversation over the phone. Or at all, if he could help it. He needed to keep Hadley off Bancroft's radar.

"Are you there?"

"Yes," he said quickly. "Are you in your office?"

"I can be in fifteen minutes."

"Great. I'll meet you there."

That would also give him time to figure out what to tell her.

"So, you are involved?"

"I didn't kill him, to answer your prior question."

"But you know something."

"I'll see you in fifteen." He ended the call. Rubbed his temples.

Why did the agent suspect him in the killing? It couldn't be based on the car alone. There were plenty of people capable of disposing the car as well as he had.

Brad squeezed the steering wheel before starting the engine.

Just as he was about to pull out of the spot, Kurt whipped around the corner.

Crackerjack timing.

Brad plastered on a smile and waved to his boss as he pulled away.

Let Kurt try and figure out what was going on. Maybe the mystery would make him more willing to talk.

If it didn't make the man more suspicious.

Neither would surprise him.

But that was the least of his concerns. Brad had to figure out what angle to go with when talking to Bancroft about Nate's disappearance. He would keep Hadley out of it unless she already knew about the connection. It was hardly a secret that his kids had been questioned in the matter. People talked, and some of the news reports had included speculations.

It was seriously time to think about moving somewhere that people didn't know them.

By the time Brad pulled into the parking lot at the

agent's building, he was no closer to knowing what to say to her.

He couldn't outright lie. She might already know the truth, at least in part.

It would be in his best interest to interrogate *her*. Figure out what she knew. He couldn't let this ruin his chances at immunity.

But he also couldn't risk bringing Hadley into the mix. He would go down before letting Bancroft anywhere near his daughter.

Once inside the office, Bancroft just stared at him. Waited for him to make the first move.

He sat. Tapped his fingers.

She did the same.

The silence between them seemed to scream.

He refused to give in.

Bancroft cracked her knuckles. "Well?"

"I already told you — I had nothing to do with the kid's disappearance."

"His murder?"

"Who said he's dead?" Brad countered. "Everyone who knows him thinks he ran away. And who could blame him? His dad's in jail for killing his mom, and his aunt is moving the kids right before his high school graduation."

She pressed her palms on the table and leaned forward. "Everything I've come across leads back to your family."

"Association doesn't mean guilt."

"It does lead one to ask questions."

"Wes Campbell — Nate's dad — has had it out for me for some time. But you have the resources to look into that. And I'm sure I don't have to tell you that he worked for the Slippery Fish before his arrest. He could still be employed by them for all I know."

"Why does he have it out for you, as you put it?"

"Because of the Slippery Fish and BlueBlade rivalry?" Brad shrugged. "How would I know? I mind my own business."

"Yet trouble seems to find you on a regular basis."

"Lately, yes."

Bancroft pulled out her tablet and slid her finger around the screen. Then she looked him in the eye. "You need to tell me the truth."

His mouth went dry, but he kept his expression steady. "I'm not lying."

"You're also not telling me the whole truth."

"What do you think I'm hiding?"

"You know something about that missing kid."

Brad flashed back to dumping his plastic-wrapped body into the harbor and kept his mouth shut.

"You do realize I can return you to the holding cell as easily as I got you out?" Bancroft asked.

"Are you threatening me?"

"I'm saying I have strings I can pull. It can go either way, and you aren't giving me much in the way of the Bergmanns."

Brad clenched his jaw.

"If you know something about that kid, you need to speak up. Your immunity is at risk."

"I do know something, but I want immunity for that person before I say anything."

Her mouth gaped slightly. "Now you're trying to broker a deal with me?"

"I'll go to prison before I let that person go."

The agent's brows drew together. "I can't offer immunity without knowing more."

"Then I can't say anything." He crossed his arms.

"You can tell me what happened."

"Can I?"

"You don't have to name names for now."

"For now?"

"After you tell me what happened, I'll tell you what I can do. It may be nothing, but perhaps I *can* provide immunity for that person. But that can't happen until I know what I'm dealing with."

Brad drew in a deep breath. Just when he thought he wouldn't have to return to the holding cell, he was looking at it as a possibility again.

"Start talking."

He gave her the bare details, careful not to say anything that might link Hadley to the murder. Also kept out any information about Faye helping with the body dump, and when discussing his own involvement, he referred to himself simply as he.

At this point, she didn't know who was involved. How long that would last was yet to be seen.

She listened, nodding occasionally and taking a few notes on her tablet.

Silence rested between them after he finished.

"And you're sure the killing was accidental?"

"Yes."

"And what about the person involved with the cover-up?"

"What about him?"

"Was that person involved in the death at all? Even slightly?"

"No. He didn't find out about it until she came to him, needing help."

"And neither of them considered going to the authorities?" Bancroft responded after a beat.

"It wasn't a possibility."

"Why not?"

"The police would never believe him."

"I see. And what about the female?"

"Too big of a risk. They might not believe her because of him."

"Really?"

"Yes! That's what happened."

The agent made some more notes. "Are you going to tell me who they are? Or do we need to play the guessing game?"

Brad sighed. "I need to know there will be immunity."

She didn't respond, her face revealed nothing.

"Well?" he asked.

"I need to know who these people are before I made a decision. I have my suspicions, but don't know if we're talking about members of your family or someone from work. That makes a difference."

"It's personal, not professional." Brad wasn't about to reveal his family's involvement just yet.

"Good." She relaxed somewhat. "Now, who are the involved parties?"

He clenched his jaw. Didn't want to give up Hadley.

"Well?"

"I want immunity for her. Otherwise, I'm not saying anything."

Bancroft's mouth formed a straight line. A storm of thoughts behind her eyes.

But she didn't say anything.

His pulse pounded.

She leaned forward. "Okay."

It took a moment to register. He stared for a moment before finding his voice. "Okay?"

"I'll make sure she has immunity. I need you for this BlueBlade job. Who is she? Is it Hadley?"

He gave a slight nod, hating himself for the act of betrayal. What if the agent decided to go back on her word? Brad could also go back on his, but what power did he have?

The agent didn't respond, didn't give any indication as to what she was thinking.

He kept the worry off his face, but each passing moment felt like an hour. Resisted the urge to ask what she thought.

A slow smile spread across her face.

Brad's stomach knotted. "What?"

She met Brad's gaze, still looking pleased. "That's something we can use."

"Meaning?"

Bancroft tapped the table. "I'm going to need some time to work out all of the details. Head back to the knife shop and work on your boss for a while. Come back here in an hour or two, and we'll talk."

"You plan on using my teenage daughter? For what?"

"We'll discuss it in an hour, once I get the details settled."

"I don't like this."

"It won't be any more dangerous than what you're doing."

"I'm deceiving a man who wants me dead and who killed my father!"

"All you need is to get information. That's it. Simple, really."

Brad groaned. "It's far more complicated than that."

"Go on. When you come back, we'll have something to discuss."

"Fine." He squeezed his fists, rose, and headed for the door.

"Before you go …"

He turned around.

"I got the results on the knife you found in your yard."

His breath hitched. "And?"

"No match on the prints, but the blood was an interesting find."

"Interesting?"

She nodded, her lips pursed. "Are you familiar with Joe Tripp?"

Brad tried to recall hearing that name. "No. Should I be?"

"No idea. But he was killed by someone associated with the Slippery Fish."

Anger rushed through him. A knife with a dead man's blood was on his property? "I had nothing to do with that."

"I know. He was murdered when you would've been a teenager."

The words nearly knocked him over. "What?"

"Like I said, interesting."

"But ... but ... if he's been dead that long, how could you match the DNA?"

"We had it on file, and someone recently ran it."

"Why?" Brad demanded.

"I didn't dig *that* deep. It was needed for another case, for comparison, I believe."

Or it was a message for Brad.

A threat of some sort.

Especially if his dad had been involved in Joe Tripp's death.

Chapter Eighteen

BRAD TURNED up the heat and glanced down the road. Faye should be home any minute.

A curtain moved across the street. No doubt the neighbors were wondering why Brad was sitting in his idling car in his own driveway.

Let them wonder. At this point it was kind of fun to wind them up. Why not, after everything they'd put him through?

A car rounded the corner.

Brad sat up straighter.

Wasn't Faye.

He slumped back down.

She'd said the salon was busy, and she was getting extra clients because of all the walk-ins. And she was taking as many as she could. Though she wasn't supposed to, she was also slipping each one her new business card for the soon-to-open home salon.

He couldn't be upset with her for being late over that.

But he did need to talk with her. Immediately.

He called her.

"Hey, Brad." Given the amount of background noise, he was on speaker.

"Are you heading home?"

"Yeah. It was crazy today, but I gave away my entire stack of cards. Tomorrow I'm putting the whole box in my car in case I run out again."

"That's great. How far are you?"

"Only about ten minutes."

Ten minutes. Too long to keep idling in the driveway.

"Let's meet at that little pizza place by the roller rink. We can bring some home for dinner."

"What's going on? Why do you want to meet?"

"We need to discuss something, and I can't risk anyone overhearing."

Not after Zeke had walked in when he was telling Hadley that he was an assassin.

"What is it?"

"Not over the phone. You'll meet me?"

"Okay." They said goodbye, and Brad headed out, calling in the order as he drove.

It would be a miracle if he could convince Faye to let Hadley go along with Agent Bancroft's plan. Brad had objected when he'd first heard her insane idea. Said he'd never let his daughter be in such a position.

But it was the only way to guarantee her immunity.

He'd already agreed, and now he needed to get Faye on board. It wouldn't be easy, but she would see that there was no other way.

Brad pulled into the parking lot just as Faye arrived from the other direction.

Luckily, the little restaurant looked fairly empty — it was still early for the dinner rush — so they could easily speak somewhere away from curious ears.

After letting the kid at the front know they were there,

he and Faye sat at a table near the back, next to a roaring fire in a large pit. The crackling would help muffle their voices even more.

Faye slid off her jacket. "What's going on?"

There was no point in beating around the bush. "The agent can offer Hadley full immunity."

His wife didn't respond, didn't even blink.

"Isn't that great news?"

"You told her about Hadley?"

"She figured it out." Sure, it was more complicated than that, but there was no point in rehashing all the details.

Faye leaned back, staring at the fire. "What's the catch?"

"Catch is a strong word. Especially considering we won't have to worry about Hadley ever getting prosecuted."

Her brows furrowed. "What do you have to do?"

"Not me."

"Hadley?" she exclaimed.

Brad nodded.

"No."

"You haven't even heard—"

"No."

Brad drew in a deep breath. He'd known this wouldn't be easy, but she wouldn't even hear him out. "She just has to take an after-school job."

Faye's expression tightened. "She's in the school play, and they rehearse after school. Aside from that, she's pregnant and grieving. Now you want to add a job on top of all that?"

"I don't want to add anything to the mix. What I do want is for her to rest easy, never having to worry about the consequences of that night ever again."

Faye shook her head.

She was already against it, and she didn't even know where Hadley would need to work.

Brad took a deep breath. "The job wouldn't be forever."

"Why would she need the job?"

He hesitated.

"Why?" Faye's eyes narrowed.

"To get a little information."

"For what?"

"Something the agent is looking into. It won't put her at any risk."

"What if she gets caught spying?"

"She won't."

Faye crossed her arms. "How can you guarantee that?"

"Because she's just going to be working, listening and watching for anything suspicious. That's it."

"You've already made up your mind."

"I'm telling you what the agent told me. It's such a small price to pay for immunity. There's also prison if—"

"Or we could keep hiding like we have been. You said there would be no chance of us being found out."

"You still believe that, even after the car was found?"

Her mouth fell open. "You don't?"

"I'm confident in my skills, but there are powerful people against me. And look what happened with the car. We can't predict everything — especially given the fact that I had zero time to prepare for any of this. It was all on the fly. We were just lucky I knew what I was doing because of my line of work."

Faye glared at him. "We don't have any other choice, do we?"

"No. Especially not now that the agent knows."

"Does she know about our involvement?"

"Mine. I left you completely out of it."

"What about your immunity?"

"It's attached to the work I'm doing now."

"Why don't *you* do the after-school work?"

"You think I can pass for a teenager?"

She frowned. "You know what I mean. Get the information yourself."

"I can't, because I'm busy with the Bergmanns. That's more than a full-time job in and of itself."

"What's the job?"

"Working a register."

She relaxed visibly. "That's it?"

"Right. And while she does that, she'll be on the lookout for anything suspicious. Anything she sees or hears, she'll report to Agent Bancroft. Easy peasy."

"Sounds *too* easy."

"We should count our blessings."

Faye ran her fingers over a scrape on the table, looking deep in thought. "And where would she be working?"

And there was the big question.

Brad tried to sound natural. "A car wash."

Her eyes widened. "The Slippery Fish?"

"That would be the one."

"Where Wes worked?"

"Right."

"And where you suspect your dad worked when he was killed?"

"Technically."

"There's no technically about it!" She glowered at him. "No way am I sending our daughter there."

"You'd rather she go to prison? I guarantee that would be a lot worse for her."

"You take the job."

"I can't."

"And why not?" she demanded.

"Ralf already ordered me to stay away from there."

The unspoken words hung in the air — Brad's life would be on the line if he took a job there.

"And yet you think it would be safe for Hadley?"

"Nobody will hurt her."

"You're sure of it?"

"It's just like the kids we hire at BlueBlade — everyone pretty much ignores them. They're just there for show, to make the business look legit. The car wash does the same thing. Nobody's going to give her a second glance."

"Except that she's your daughter, and gorgeous. Everyone's going to notice her."

"It isn't ideal, I'll be the first to admit that."

"Really? Because that's the first I'm hearing you admit to anything of the sort."

He counted silently. "All I can say is that this is far better than prison, far better than her worrying every time someone looks at her funny or the doorbell rings. This will allow her to move on and live a normal life. That's all we want for her, right?"

"You do realize she's never going to have a normal life, don't you? Her dad is an assassin, she accidentally killed one of her friends, and she's going to have her dead boyfriend's baby."

"But this will give her the best shot possible. She can move on from her mistakes and make better decisions without worrying about going to prison for life. That will be a huge weight off her shoulders."

They sat in silence.

He might need to give her the chance to sleep on it, to see that there was no other way.

Brad's name rang out over the loudspeaker.

He pushed the chair back. "I'll grab the pizzas."

Faye nodded, not looking at him.

"She'll be fine."

No response.

He paid for the food and waited for Faye to join him.

She still sat in her seat, staring at the fire.

Brad carried the boxes over and set them on the table. "You ready?"

"I have another idea."

He held back a groan. "What is it?"

"I'll take the job."

It was a good thing he'd already put the pizzas on the table. He surely would've dropped them otherwise. "Excuse me?"

She held his gaze. "You heard me. I'll take the job."

He shook his head.

"And why not?"

"Because that isn't the deal."

"So, negotiate. That way, Hadley won't have to deal with those criminals."

"You don't think that will raise suspicions?"

"About what?"

Brad collapsed onto the chair. The aromas from the pizzas made his mouth water. "You mean, other than the fact that Kurt just paid for your home salon? It's hardly a secret that you're opening it. There's a connection between the two companies — even though I don't know what it is yet — but what I do know is, word will travel. And fast."

She shrugged. "My salon is slow to take off. I have to supplement my income. Makes perfect sense."

He wrung his hands together.

"What's wrong with that plan?"

"Hadley will be a lot less conspicuous. It's a job for high school and college kids."

She leaned back. "You don't think I can do it."

"I think it will raise too many eyebrows."

"At least it would put Hadley out of harm's way! Something only I seem concerned about."

"I don't have a lot of leeway. If we want Hadley to receive immunity, she has to do the work."

"She's a *minor*. There's no reason one of us can't step in for her. Unless there's something you aren't telling me."

"I've already explained it to you. We can't let word get back to the Bergmanns that one of us is working at the car wash. Can you imagine Kurt's reaction after spending all that money on your salon? There's no way he would trust me if either of us work there."

"And you think your daughter working there will be any better?"

"Yes."

"How?" she demanded.

"Because she's just a kid! I can claim that I didn't know about her applying for the job. But if either one of us takes it, I can't say that. It has to be her. Not only did she commit the crime, Hadley's the only one who can do this, to earn her immunity."

Faye scowled.

"Do you see my point?"

"I don't like it."

"Neither do I."

"Have you told our daughter about this yet?"

"No. I wanted to speak with you first."

"Great. We'll break the news to her after dinner."

Faye got up and left without another word.

Chapter Nineteen

BRAD PUT AWAY the last box of inventory and glanced over at Kurt's office. The door was closed, but at least his boss was in for the day. He'd managed several brief conversations, but had no idea if Kurt was starting to believe Brad had given up on his search for his father's killer, or if he remained suspicious.

And that made it all the harder for Brad to carry on with the charade. Was he overdoing the theatrics? Or was it the right amount of kissing up?

Time would tell, but with Bancroft checking in on him constantly, time was yet another enemy marching against him. That woman wanted results, and she wanted them yesterday.

If only he could go back in time and make different decisions, how much better everything would be.

He'd never get into the assassination business, for starters. If he hadn't been so obsessed with his career, he might've seen the signs of his oldest dating a grown man right under his nose. She wouldn't be pregnant, and Duke wouldn't be dead — since his death was meant to make

Brad look guilty. If none of that would've happened, Faye wouldn't have become friends with Allison and Hadley wouldn't have had any reason to talk to Nate. Wes might still have killed Allison, but Nate would be alive.

His intentions had been good — wanting to escape financial ruin and to help make the world a better place — but he should've known there would be grave consequences for jumping into such a career. If only he hadn't been so blinded by anger. And so desperate to fight back against the kind of people who'd stolen his father from him.

"Earth to Brad."

He turned in the direction of the voice.

Kurt.

"I just got done with the inventory."

"Good. Come in." Kurt motioned for him to come into the office.

Finally.

Now it was time to put his acting skills to the test.

"How is the salon working out for Faye?" Kurt closed the door behind them and took his seat on the other side of the desk.

Brad made himself comfortable in the other chair while looking around the room without making it obvious. "She can't wait to open it."

"She hasn't yet?"

"She had to give notice at work, but it's for the best anyway. Faye's been able to pass out her new business cards to clients in the meantime."

"And your mom?"

"She's doing well."

"I mean, where is she during the day, if your wife and you are both at work?"

"At an adult daycare center."

He lifted a brow. "Was that not an option before? I was under the impression that the only—"

"The availability came up suddenly, and isn't permanent. We definitely need — and appreciate — the salon and how quickly you were able to make that happen. You were a real lifesaver." Sucking up made Brad want to dig and hole and crawl into it.

"Since you're back to work, it's time for another target. Don't you think?"

"I thought you'd never ask." Brad studied him, trying to figure out his angle. This was definitely a test, but what kind?

Kurt opened his laptop and tapped the keys, staring at the screen.

Brad took advantage of his distraction to look around the perimeter. For anywhere Kurt might be hiding records too incriminating to keep online — anywhere beyond the obvious.

Nothing stood out as a clear hiding spot. There were a few framed pictures large enough to be hiding a safe, or they could just be pictures. A shelf full of books that could be hollowed out to hold secrets, or even marked in code. If Brad checked all the ceiling tiles, would he find a secret cache behind one of them?

No, those were all incredibly obvious. Anything he'd seen on TV was probably an awful hiding place. Same for all those things you could buy in a surplus military store or spy supply shop online. Clever enough to fool an amateur, but not nearly secure enough for someone like Kurt.

And Brad was assuming that Kurt wouldn't put his operation's records any place that could be hacked. What if he'd invested in serious encryption, or created some sort of vault on the dark web that couldn't be hacked?

Then Brad would be spending the rest of his life in prison.

And so would Hadley.

He was betting both their futures on the belief that Kurt and Ralf were too old-school to rely on tech to protect their records.

Kurt interrupted his thoughts. "This one is going to involve travel."

"Okay." Brad struggled to steady his expression. "Where to?"

Kurt didn't reply right away.

The silence made Brad's stomach do somersaults. He made fists in his lap, where his boss couldn't see. Didn't let any emotion leak to his face.

"It'll be out of country this time."

This was a suicide mission, on foreign soil. "Been a while since I've had one of those."

"That won't be a problem, will it?"

Brad forced a grin. "I love the challenge."

"Where is the target?"

One side of Kurt's mouth curved slightly. "Somewhere in Europe — we think. You'll have to figure that out on your own."

"The bigger the challenge, the better."

"That's why you're one of our top guys."

They stared each other down, both feigning pleasure.

"What crime did our guy commit?"

"Cult leader." Kurt didn't miss a beat. "Got away after inciting a mass suicide in Honduras. Intel says he's got a new group gathered."

His boss was a phenomenal liar, Brad had to give him that.

"And you think he's in Europe now?"

"That's what we believe."

"You can't even narrow it down to a country?"

Kurt leaned forward. "I *could*, but why waste my time when we have someone like you on the job?"

Brad's stomach lurched as Kurt returned his attention to the laptop. "I just emailed you the information."

"No file?"

"Not this time."

"Are we moving to a new system?"

"Sure." Kurt stood and motioned toward the door. "I'll let you go. I'm sure Josh could use the help at the front of the store. We're a little understaffed today."

"Of course. I'll look into the target later."

"Perfect."

Brad forced a smile, scanning the office again as he left.

The agent would not be happy — not only had Brad failed to persuade Kurt to trust him again, he'd made sure that there wouldn't be any reason to hang around the shop.

But that wasn't the worst part. Kurt had asked about Faye and his mother, which meant he probably planned to go after them next.

How was he supposed to protect his family from an ocean away?

His mind raced as he worked the sales floor on autopilot, managing to sell several pricey sets despite the fact that his mind was elsewhere.

Josh stared at him in disbelief. "How are you able to do that? I tell people the same things you do, but they just buy from the bargain bin."

"It's all in the presentation. I've had years of practice."

Brad made a show of offering the kid some pointers, because Kurt was surely watching on the security cameras.

Bancroft texted and called a few times while he was in the showroom, increasing the pressure already building.

Once it was time for his lunch break, Brad hightailed it

to his car for some privacy. His stomach was too balled up to eat any of the food he'd packed, but he checked his email for the information on his new target, then called the agent back.

"Why have you been ignoring my calls?" she demanded.

"You have me working at a knife shop. I can't be on the phone while on the clock."

"What progress did you make with Bergmann?"

"Kurt wants me dead. My family, too."

"He said that?"

"Not in so many words."

She sighed on the other end of the line. "What *did* he say in so many words?"

"He asked about my wife and mom — that was definitely a threat. Then he gave me a new target in Europe."

"They're sending you across the world? For what?"

"To kill a 'cult leader.' No idea what the real story is. Haven't had time to do any digging."

"What's his name?"

Brad went back to the email. "Giuliano Franco."

"Are you messing with me?"

"No. Why would I?"

"Under no circumstance are you to kill that man."

Pressure built behind Brad's temples. "Who is he?"

"The wealthy son of a politician in Italy. Very influential. Has ties to other political leaders around the world, including here in the US."

"Why have I never heard of him?"

"Because he gets more accomplished without the spotlight. But those details aren't important. All you need to know is, don't go near the man."

"What am I supposed to tell my boss?"

"Whatever you need to. Pretend to look into him."

"He wants me to travel. And like I said, he threatened my family. I'll have to worry about my mom and wife. My kids, too, even though Kurt hasn't threatened them yet. Especially once he gets wind of Hadley working at the car wash."

"She starts work tomorrow."

"Hadley?"

"Yes. Make sure she shows up at three-thirty."

"You can guarantee her safety?" Brad swallowed hard.

"Yes. I have people watching your family. Let me handle everything — your daughter, your wife, your mother. All you need to do is get that information from the Bergmanns. That's the only thing I want on your mind. Nothing else."

Brad drew in a deep breath. "I need more time."

"Do I need to send someone in your place?" Her tone sharpened. "Do you miss that holding cell?"

"No," he snapped. "If I don't play this right, Kurt will never trust me enough to let me get close to those files."

"Then you're going to have to resort to other measures."

"You want me to break into his office?"

"Or his house."

"Do you know the kind of security he has?" Brad exclaimed. "These people are loaded."

"It's up to you, the easy way or the hard way."

He tugged on his hair. "What do you suggest I do when he tries to send me to Italy, or wherever Giuliano Franco is?"

"Get the information before then."

Of course. What an easy answer.

"Are we on the same page, Morris?"

"Yes."

139

"Talk to you soon. I hope for your sake that you'll have good news for me."

Brad didn't respond before she ended the call.

There was no way he could get the information she wanted.

Not before Kurt managed to kill him, and his family.

Chapter Twenty

HADLEY STARED at the kids around the lunch table. It sounded like they were all speaking foreign languages. She couldn't comprehend a word.

Now she had to take on an after-school job on top of everything else. At least that gave her an answer about quitting the play. Not that it was really up for debate. She hadn't been practicing her lines at all.

The good news was that if she took the job, she wouldn't ever go to jail for what happened to Nate. A much better price to pay than going to prison.

Most anything would be.

Not that it would stop kids at school from being suspicious. All day, they'd stared and whispered. Some of the bolder ones had asked her directly if she had anything to do with Nate's disappearance. Only one guy had the nerve to ask her if she killed him. To her face, at least. She'd heard the whispers.

She'd been saved by the bell, literally, but her luck wouldn't last.

Even if she was given immunity, it wouldn't take away the fact that she was actually guilty. She still had to live with what she'd done.

Laughter sounded all around Hadley, bringing her back to the present, to the table in the cafeteria.

Ellie was looking directly at her. Staring. Nostrils flared and brows furrowed.

Hurt and anger burned in Hadley's chest.

She grabbed her tray, stepped back from the table, and stormed away from her friends — especially her now former best friend — without saying anything.

Virtual school was sounding better by the minute.

She dumped the tray before hurrying into the hallway.

That stupid social worker stood across the hall.

Maybe the immunity would get her to quit visiting the school.

If only the job started now, during school hours. That would be a dream come true. Getting away from all of these people who accused her. The same ones who used to adore her.

How far she'd fallen. People used to copy everything she did — from outfits she put together to new ways of doing her makeup. Now they shrunk back in horror. Like they could catch a deadly disease.

Hadley turned around and hurried down the hall to avoid the social worker.

A group of gamer geeks pointed and snickered.

She darted down another corridor.

Some burnouts were gathered in a corner, huddled around something she couldn't see. They called out accusations. Names. One threatened her.

Hadley blinked back tears and ran for the nearest exit, but stopped before reaching it. She needed to leave and never return. That meant emptying out her locker.

It was halfway across the building, and the halls were filled with kids finishing the lunch period. Soon the bell would ring.

Her best bet would be to hide out until the next period began. Then she could make it to her locker without incident, empty her personal items into her bag — the textbooks could stay — and make her way to her car.

And never return.

She made her way to a classroom she knew to be empty and pressed herself against a wall, just out of view of the large windows.

The first bell rang.

Hadley held her breath as conversation sounded from the hall — people laughed and joked, something slammed against the window. She used to be part of all that fun.

Those days were over. Now that she had killed Nate.

He deserved to be out there with the others more than she did.

The lump in her throat choked her. She slid down to sit on the floor. Fought off the tears. Didn't last long. Rested her forehead on her knees and gave into the heaving sobs.

While she felt horrible about not being part of all the fun anymore, Nate didn't have the option to feel anything. Unless he was somewhere watching. In that case, maybe he was in a better place.

Or maybe he wanted her to pay.

She shuddered at the thought.

The next bell rang.

Conversation and laughter quickly waned as everyone rushed into their classrooms, but Hadley waited.

Hall monitors would be on the lookout for straggling kids who were avoiding class.

The seconds on the clock dragged on in slow motion.

She wiped tears that she was barely aware were still

falling. Glanced out the window, and seeing nobody, ran over to the teacher's desk and yanked tissues from the box. Rushed back to her hiding spot and blew her nose, only for more tears to come.

The stiff tissues scratched her skin. She threw them into the trash before peeking out the windows.

No hall monitors.

Heart pounding, she cracked open the door. Poked her head out.

Still nobody.

She darted out and hurried down the eerily quiet hall. The only sounds were the muffled lectures of teachers behind closed doors.

Each time she passed a classroom, she slowed and held her head high, walking as though she were supposed to be there. She ducked into a bathroom when voices sounded around a corner. Had to leap into a stall and stand on a toilet when someone came inside. Waited for the sounds of someone relieving herself before fleeing.

Her heart felt like it would give out by the time she finally reached her locker. With sweaty palms, she spun the code to open it. Yanked textbooks from her bag and stuffed them inside. Then pulled her makeup bag and other necessities from the locker to where the textbooks had been.

The only things left were the photos she'd stuck on the inside of the door. Images of her and Ellie laughing and making funny faces — they mocked her now. Reminded her of good times that would never return.

More tears stung.

She reached for pictures taken with other friends. But most of them had been at the lunch table laughing at her.

None of those people mattered anymore.

She sure didn't matter to them now.

Taking a shaky breath, she slammed the locker shut for the last time.

Instantly regretted closing it so loudly. Her action would draw attention from anyone nearby.

Hadley glanced around before hurrying around a corner and making her way to the nearest exit, avoiding as many classrooms as possible.

Finally made it to the parking lot.

Then to her car.

Someone shouted behind her. Called out her name.

It was her second period teacher.

Hadley unlocked her car as she ran, then leaped in and tossed her bag onto the passenger seat. Started the engine and peeled out of the parking spot. Out of the parking lot.

To freedom.

The teacher could call her parents, but they would understand. They wouldn't object to her signing up for virtual school, so she wouldn't have to deal with all the idiotic drama.

At least she had the house to herself. Everyone else was at work or school, except for Grandma, who seemed to be having a lot of fun hanging out with her new friends.

Hadley kicked off her shoes, dropped her bag, and went into the kitchen. She hadn't touched her disgusting school lunch, and now she was famished.

After scarfing down the remains of a casserole, she went to the couch and found a mindless movie to stream. It was such a relief not having to worry about homework.

But the TV wasn't enough of a distraction. Every guy on the screen made her think of either Duke or Nate.

She rubbed her stomach, wondering if seeing the baby would help ease the pain of losing Duke. Or would it make it worse? Seemed like it could go either way.

Nothing would make her feel better about the kid she had killed.

What if she still felt overwhelming guilt, even after spying at the car wash for that agent?

Would a confession be the only thing to quell her screaming conscience?

Chapter Twenty-One

FAYE GLANCED up at the clock. Again. Not even two minutes had passed since last checking the time. It was impossible to keep her mind on the task at hand. She kept picturing Hadley at the car wash, getting roughed up by some assassin thug. Someone worse than Wes had been.

She checked the length of her client's hair. The back was uneven. By a lot.

"You almost done?" Jadyn gave her a sweet smile, but it didn't reach her eyes. "I have an appointment after this."

"Just making some final touches." Faye gave her an equally syrupy smile. "Wouldn't want you walking away with anything less than perfect."

"Doesn't usually take this long." Her tone dripped of judgment.

"Can't rush something as important as hair." Faye snipped a bit off the back. Compared it to the rest. "Your hair is pretty dry — brittle on the ends from the constant coloring."

"That's what maintenance trims are for. Your job to fix

it." Jadyn glanced back down at her phone and tapped the screen rapidly with her thumbs.

Faye bit back a snarky comment. She could be the bigger person. She would be.

Or she might not be. Her nerves were worn down by the lack of sleep and constant worries.

"What did you just do?" Jadyn shrieked.

Faye looked back and forth between the chunk of hair in her hand and the gaping spot in the back of the twenty-something's hair.

Jadyn yanked off the cape, tearing it. "My hair is ruined!"

She held a hand mirror behind her back and looked at the disaster from the reflection on the wall mirror.

Everyone else was staring — other stylists and clients alike. Every eye in the place was focused on her.

Faye could either apologize and make quick work of the mess or she could flee.

She chose option two.

Ran into the back room, heart thundering. Collapsed onto the loveseat and tried to catch her breath. Tried to care about the brat's hair. Couldn't bring herself to.

Cheryl entered the room. "Why aren't you out there? You need to fix her hair!"

Faye rose. "I quit. You'll have to find someone else to take the rest of my clients for today and beyond."

"You can't do this!"

"Watch me."

Cheryl started to say something, but Faye spun around and flung open her locker, making so much noise that she didn't have to listen to the lecture. She gathered her things and stormed out of the room. Marched through the salon, making eye contact with no one.

A flurry of voices ran through the room.

Didn't matter. Once she left, she would never have to return again.

She never should've bothered giving her notice. Should've quit on the spot, as soon as her home salon was ready.

By the time she reached her driveway, tears had obliterated her makeup. It wasn't until she got out of the car that she noticed Hadley's car next to the sidewalk.

What was she doing home? Brad must've given permission for her to leave. Hopefully she wasn't sick. No. Nix that. Hopefully she *was*. Then she wouldn't have to go to that ridiculous after-school job. Faye could take her place.

A car driving by slowed down. The windows were tinted, so the driver was hidden.

A nosy neighbor? Or was that social worker back again? Faye waved, staring directly at the driver's side, letting them know that they weren't fooling her.

The car picked up speed and drove on.

Their neighbors would always view the family as guilty of something, despite Brad being proved innocent of every accusation. Soon Hadley would be publicly cleared.

Then they would have peace.

It was hard to believe how much everything had changed over the course of a few months. It felt like a year. A decade, even.

She pushed those thoughts aside and hurried into the house.

Quiet.

"Hadley?"

No response.

Faye kicked off her shoes and dumped her things on a couch in the front room before looking through the downstairs, not finding her daughter.

STACY CLAFLIN & NOLON KING

Hadley was at her desk, typing furiously on her computer.

"Are you sick?"

She jumped and turned. "Mom! Don't scare me like that."

"What are you doing home from school already?"

"I'm signing up for virtual school. What are *you* doing home so early?"

"I quit my job to focus on *my* salon."

"Sounds good." Hadley turned back to the computer. "From what I could find, there are a few virtual school options. I'll have to get your signature or Dad's."

Faye leaned against the door frame. "We'll figure that out later."

"Considering I quit school without telling the office, we probably have to make it quick."

"You left without informing anyone?"

"I can't deal with it there. It's too much. Everyone thinks it's my fault that Nate is gone. Some of them think I killed him!"

Faye wrapped her arms around Hadley. "You don't have to go back. We've been talking about virtual school or homeschool. Now it's a reality instead of a possibility. We'll get it figured out, but not right now. I need to call Dad and let him know what's going on."

"He won't answer."

"How do you know?"

"Because I've been calling both of you, and neither of you are answering. Good thing it wasn't an emergency." Hadley gave her mother an accusatory glare.

"Fair enough, but you know I'm not allowed to take calls when I'm with a client."

"I called like five times."

150

"My new rule is that I have to answer every phone call, even when I'm with a client. I think I'm going to like being my own boss."

Hadley picked up her phone and frowned.

"What's wrong?"

"Kids are texting me about Nate. Nonstop."

"Block them. You don't go to school with them anymore."

"Yeah, but people are still going to talk on social media."

"Block them there, too."

"I'm always going to be the girl who killed Nate. Doesn't matter if I block people or not. This is going to follow me forever."

"I know it feels like the end of the world, but life will move on. Some new story will distract people, and soon they'll forget all about you."

"That's supposed to help me feel better?"

"Yes, actually."

"Don't ever get a job as a motivational speaker."

Faye pulled up a chair and sat next to her. "What will help you feel better?"

"Going back in time and changing *everything* that has happened this year."

"Let me rephrase my question. What in the realm of possibility will help you feel better?"

Hadley shrugged again.

"Imagine everything worked out for the best, what would that be like?"

Tears shone in her eyes. "Duke and Nate would be alive again."

"Again, realm of possibility."

"For everyone to leave me alone and stop being mean."

"Maybe after a few weeks of virtual schooling, that'll happen."

Hadley snorted. "Right."

"You don't think so?"

"No."

"What do you want to do? You aren't giving me anything to work with."

Silence rested between them.

"I should confess."

Faye nearly fell out of her chair. "What? I thought we were past this nonsense."

"It isn't nonsense. I killed Nate!"

"And you're about to get immunity. All you have to do is work at a car wash." Faye couldn't believe she was encouraging Hadley to take the job.

"But that won't change the fact that I actually did it. That I'm going to feel guilty for the rest of my life."

"Confessing won't fix that. You can't change the past. There's no sense in wasting the rest of your years behind bars. Do this for Nate. For Duke."

Hadley looked at her like she was crazy. "For Nate and Duke?"

"They aren't able to live out the rest of their lives as they should. Live yours to the fullest, for the both of them."

Hadley frowned.

Would it work? They'd had this conversation before — if knowing that her confession would also send her parents to prison wouldn't convince Hadley to stay quiet, what would?

Would they have to take away her electronics indefinitely?

Keep her locked in her room until Brad could fix this mess?

With any luck, Hadley would forget the idea of confessing.

Faye didn't want to think about what would happen if she didn't.

Chapter Twenty-Two

BRAD STARED at his house from inside the car, said goodbye to Bancroft, and ended the call. He was starting to think he'd have to attempt breaking and entering if he wanted to stay out of prison.

But for now, all he wanted was to go inside, have something warm to eat with his family, and kick up his feet for a while. At least he wouldn't have to spend any time looking up information on his target. Bancroft had already emailed some info he could regurgitate to Kurt the next morning so it would look like he'd done some serious digging. Meanwhile, he planned to binge-watch something with Faye and let his problems percolate in the back of his head.

He got out of the car and trudged up to the porch. Leaned against a railing, trying to build the energy to make it inside. His muscles ached and his head pounded. He could fall asleep where he stood.

But he took a deep breath and forced himself to make the last few steps to the door. Mouthwatering aromas made his stomach growl as he entered. His plan to eat and chill was looking good.

He followed the scents to the kitchen, where his mom stirred something on the stove. Faye was chopping carrots.

"How is everyone?" he asked.

Faye turned, her eyes wide. "Hadley and I have been trying to get ahold of you."

He rubbed his eyes. "I saw that, but you won't believe the drama I'm dealing with. Kurt wants me to go to Italy to—"

He stopped short, realizing his mom was in the room.

"Italy?" Faye exclaimed.

"To look at knives?" his mom asked.

"Something like that." Brad motioned to the other room, looking at Faye. "Can we talk?"

His mom put down the spoon. "You two go ahead. I'll add the carrots to the stew."

"Thanks." Faye smiled at her but spoke to Brad. "What's this about Italy?"

"Come on." He pulled her into the living room, but Luna was watching a movie, so they went to their room instead.

"You're going to Italy?" Faye looked at him like he was crazy.

"Chances are, I'm not leaving this time."

"Because of the agent?"

"Right. She's ordered me not to kill my target, and yet Kurt expects nothing less."

"What are you going to do?"

"If I want to stay out of prison, I'm not killing the guy."

Her eyes widened. "Will you have to make Kurt think you killed him?"

"No idea. But if I can get to the information Bancroft wants, then it'll be a moot point."

"How close are you?"

"At this point, not very."

Faye frowned. "What's it going to take?"

He wrung his hands together. "I've been trying to figure this out all day. Can we discuss something else? Like dinner."

"Or the fact that I quit the salon today."

"Good for you." He nodded in approval.

"It wasn't good! I screwed up on someone's hair because I couldn't concentrate."

"Were you worried about my job?"

"I was worried about *Hadley*." Her brows furrowed. "We're throwing her into a lions' den, and you're doing nothing to protect her."

Brad rubbed his temples. "The agent has people watching us. Hadley will be fine — her job won't be like mine. I have to get to the Bergmanns' secret files. She just has to listen for any information dropped. She'll probably spend the entire time pushing buttons and making change."

Faye's mouth formed a straight line.

"Considering she's going to get immunity for killing someone, we don't have much to complain about. Any other family would be betting on whatever lawyer they could afford."

"You should've done a better job of covering up the murder!"

Anger surged through him, making it hard to find a clear thought. He drew a deep breath and held her gaze. "First of all, it wasn't *murder*. She didn't premeditate anything. Second, I did the best I could, without time to prepare. And third, I did a phenomenal job. Nobody can prove we had anything to do with it. You should be thanking me."

"If it's such a sure thing, then why bother with immunity?"

"Why bother with insurance?"

She glowered at him.

He glared back.

Ding-dong!

"Crackerjack timing," he grumbled.

"Expecting anyone?" Faye crossed her arms.

"No. You?"

Her only response was to head into the hall.

Brad caught up and passed her before reaching the stairs. If anyone was going to deal with whoever was at the door, it was going to be him.

He didn't even bother checking before flinging the door open.

Detective Stewart.

Brad resisted the urge to slam the door back shut. "What do you want?"

"Hello to you, too."

"You can't arrest me. I haven't done anything wrong — it was already proven."

"I'm not here to speak to you."

He stepped closer. "Who, then?"

"Hadley."

"No."

"We have some questions for her."

"Now isn't a good time."

"That's too bad, because she's coming to the station for questioning."

"No, she isn't."

"Do the words *reasonable suspicion* mean anything to you?"

Those words meant that Detective Stewart could detain Hadley for questioning, and that she was confident she had enough evidence that a judge would find the detention legal.

She might even have enough to get a warrant, if Brad continued to refuse.

At which point there would be nothing he could do to stop her.

They stared each other down, Brad's anger nearly reaching a boiling point.

Right now, all he could do was damage control — tell Hadley to lawyer up and keep her mouth shut until he could get Bancroft to intervene.

The detective spoke first. "We're questioning her whether you like it or not. Your only say in the matter is whether I drive her or you do."

Brad clenched his fists. "You know the answer to that one."

"Great. I'll wait while you get her."

He resisted the urge to punch something. Turned to Faye. "Get Hadley. I'll call my attorney."

Detective Stewart didn't budge from her spot on the porch.

"You don't have to wait for us."

"I think I will."

"Have fun with that." He closed the door between them and locked it. Tapped out a text to Agent Bancroft as he made his way to the kitchen to let his mother know that they were leaving. Zeke would have to keep an eye on her.

She glanced at him from the stove. "Ready for stew?"

His stomach rumbled. He thought about the detective outside. "Don't mind if I do. But it's going to have to be quick. Faye and I need to take Hadley somewhere."

She hesitated. "What's wrong?"

"It'll be fine."

"That doesn't answer my question."

"No, you don't need to worry." He poured himself some stew and dug in, burning his mouth and not caring.

Faye came into the kitchen and glared at him. "You're eating?"

"I'm hungry."

"So am I." Hadley pushed past her mom and scooped stew into a bowl for herself.

Faye put her hands on her hips. "She's waiting out there, you know."

Brad swallowed. "Yep."

"And you don't care?" Faye exclaimed. "If we make her wait too long, that could make things worse for Hadley."

"That won't affect anything," Brad said.

"Who's waiting?" his mom asked.

He put his hand on her shoulder. "Nothing for you to worry about."

"I'm not a child, son."

"Of course not. But the only thing you need to worry about is what cartoon to watch with Luna."

She frowned.

Faye shot icy glares at Brad.

He swallowed. "I'm almost done."

"Me too," Hadley chimed in.

Brad's phone buzzed.

Bancroft, agreeing to meet them at the station.

Now he just needed to make sure that Hadley kept it together for a few more hours.

Chapter Twenty-Three

BRAD PULLED INTO A PARKING SPOT, but didn't cut the engine. Turned back to Hadley. "Let's go over this one last time."

She rolled her eyes. "Seriously?"

"You want to stay out of prison?"

Hadley sighed dramatically. "Don't say anything unless the agent says I can."

"Don't call her an agent in there."

"I'll call her a lawyer, just like you said. Can we go in and get this over with? I just want to get back home."

"This is *serious*," Faye snapped. "Getting back to watch *Hollywood Housewives* isn't our concern here."

"That show is so three years ago, Mom."

"Enough." Brad checked his phone and looked around for the agent's car.

"It looks like the detective is waiting for us," Faye said.

"She can go inside if she wants."

"I'm sure she wants to see us come in with her own eyes. If anyone is a flight risk, it's us."

Brad looked at Faye in disbelief. "If we were a flight

risk, we wouldn't have been home when she showed up. We'd be out of the country. She knows they have nothing on Hadley. The woman is grasping for straws."

"Purposefully annoying her isn't going to help Hadley."

"No, Agent Bancroft will do that for us."

She opened the door. "I'm going to speak with her. Someone needs to show the detective that we're willing to cooperate."

"We're here, aren't we?"

"And you're being as difficult as possible about this. Hadley wants to get home, and I don't blame her."

"You just said—"

"I'm going to talk with the detective." Faye got out and slammed the door before Brad could respond. What did she think she was going to say that would make this better?

"Are you going after her?" Hadley asked.

"No." He checked his phone again. "Why don't you seem more nervous?"

"You just got done telling me I don't have to say anything."

"Unless the agent tells you to," he clarified.

"What's she going to let me say? We all know I did it. I've seen enough TV to know how this works."

"This isn't TV." Brad glanced over at Faye and Stewart. They were speaking under a light near the entrance to the station.

If Brad never had to return to this building, it would be too soon.

Hadley maneuvered herself into the front passenger seat. "Looking at the two of them, you'd think they were only discussing the weather."

"She's trying to protect you."

"I thought you two were arguing. Now you're defending her?"

"Pointing out facts. Seriously, why are you so much less stressed than you have been?"

Hadley put her feet on the dash. "It's such a relief knowing I won't have to go to school and deal with everyone talking about this tomorrow."

"You aren't going to school in the morning?"

She gave him a funny look. "I decided I'm not going back ever. Didn't Mom tell you?"

"We barely had time to discuss her quitting before the detective showed up."

"You should be happy. Now the two of us will be home all day to help with Grandma."

Brad shook his head. "Grandma's happy at the center, and you two will be busy. You're going to focus on virtual school and Mom has a business to run."

Hadley sighed.

Lights from a car turning into the parking lot shined on them.

Brad leaned forward, trying to tell if it was Agent Bancroft.

It was.

"Is it showtime?" Hadley asked.

"Yes."

"Should I act confident? Or nervous? What do you think will help me look innocent?"

"Are you looking at this like a role in a school play?"

She chewed on her lower lip. "It's the only way I'm able to hold myself together."

He leaned over and wrapped his arms around her. "It's all going to be fine. Be as truthful as you can without admitting anything that will make you look guilty. Same story as it's been all along — you had a disagreement with Nate at school but didn't see him after that. But make sure the agent gives the okay before you say a word. There won't be anything wrong with you not saying a word to the detective."

"Okay. So, what's my angle? Nervous Nelly, Confident Connie, or—?"

"Sweet and innocent. It wouldn't hurt to say something about how you have nothing to hide when the agent tells you not to say something. Just don't overdo it."

"That should be easy enough." She fidgeted with her coat zipper. "Do I need to talk to the agent first? Tell her what happened?"

"She already knows."

Brad hurried over to Bancroft and introduced her to Hadley before they all made their way over to Faye and the detective.

Stewart led them to an interrogation room.

"We want to speak with our attorney in private." Brad gestured toward the two-way mirror, letting the detective know he knew what it was. "I want another room first."

She sighed like he was really putting her out.

Bancroft nodded in agreement. "I'm going to have to insist on that."

"Fine." Stewart led them to a small room where they would barely have room to sit. "I'll be back in fifteen minutes."

The four of them squeezed inside and sat around the table.

Brad turned to the agent. "What's the plan?"

"I need to find out what they know — if anything. This could just be a ploy, in hopes that one of you will tell them what they want to hear."

Once back in the interrogation room, Hadley got right into character. At least the girl was a first-class actress, always landing her school's lead roles. Who would have guessed it would pay off like this?

Stewart looked at Brad and Faye. "You'll need to leave."

"She's a minor." Faye turned to Brad. "She can't make us leave, can she?"

Bancroft nodded. "Hadley's in good hands, I promise."

Faye grabbed Brad's arm.

"Let's go."

She pleaded with her eyes.

Like that would do any good.

Brad squeezed her hand and led her out of the room.

"How can they do this?" Faye asked.

"As long as she follows the agent's lead, everything will be fine." He held the door for her to the waiting room, and they sat in stiff plastic seats.

Faye grimaced. "Do I want to know why the seats are plastic?"

"Probably not."

"I can't wait for the day that our lives will no longer be interrupted by police visits."

"You and me both."

Faye tapped the seat and glanced around the room, obviously trying to avoid looking at the guy with long greasy hair, a gaping wound on his arm, and fishnet stockings.

Brad's phone rang.

"Is that the agent?" Faye asked.

"Don't know why she'd call." He dug out his phone and checked the screen.

Kurt.

He held back an annoyed comment as he answered. "Brad here."

"Have you started looking into our guy?"

"I'm working on it as we speak."

"Right now?"

164

Brad hesitated. Did Kurt know he was at the police station? If he thought Brad had turned on him, he'd send every available assassin after their family. "You don't believe me?"

"Just asking a question."

"You know I take my assignments seriously. Always have."

"Yes." Kurt paused. "How's it coming?"

"These things take time. I can fill you in on the details in the morning."

"Make sure you get plenty of rest."

"Will do."

"And be sure you've made plenty of progress on Franco by morning. I want a detailed report."

"Consider it done."

"Buh-bye."

The call ended.

Faye lifted a brow. "What was that about?"

"That's what I need to find out."

"What do you mean?"

"He was acting strange. Possibly insinuating that he knows where we are."

Her mouth gaped. "How?"

"Likely knows someone who works here."

She looked up for a moment before making eye contact again. "You don't think he's behind Detective Stewart's sudden confidence about questioning Hadley?"

"Nothing would surprise me at this point."

"You need to get out of that business."

"That's the plan."

They waited in silence until Bancroft escorted Hadley into the waiting room.

"Done already?" Brad asked.

"Finally!" Faye leaped up and threw her arms around Hadley. "I was so worried about you!"

"She did great." Bancroft smiled at Hadley before turning to Brad. "Let's head outside where we can talk."

Brad could barely pull Faye away from their daughter to get to the parking lot. "How did it go?"

"Great." Bancroft pulled out her tablet and looked at the screen. "It's as I suspected — the police have nothing to go on other than hunches. Kids keep bringing up the disagreement Hadley had with Nate the night he disappeared, but that hardly proves anything."

"I didn't have to say anything. Just played my part." Hadley smiled.

Faye wrapped her arms around her and turned to the agent. "Are they going to leave us alone now?"

"Yes." She turned her attention back to the screen. "And to set your mind at ease, we have a fall guy."

Brad's heart skipped a beat. "You have someone to take the blame?"

"Yes."

"How did you manage that?" Faye exclaimed.

The agent glanced at her. "All you need to know is that he's guilty of far worse than this, but was never caught. Your concern is making sure Hadley shows up at the car wash for her job."

The two of them continued speaking, but Brad couldn't concentrate.

Someone else was going down for the killing.

Chapter Twenty-Four

BRAD DOWNED the rest of his coffee — his third cup of the morning — and tossed the paper cup into the trash before following Kurt into his office. Stifling a yawn and ignoring the urge to rub the back of his sore neck, he sat in the chair opposite his boss.

"Busy night, huh?" Kurt put his hands behind his head and stared down his nose at Brad.

Did he know about the police station?

Had he been behind it?

None of this should surprise him, but he was so exhausted, he was starting to lose his edge. All he needed was one good night of sleep. Or maybe a week.

"Not feeling talkative?" One corner of Kurt's mouth curved up slightly.

Goosebumps ran down Brad's back. "I'd rather discuss how I can move up in the company."

"Move up? I didn't realize you had aspirations to go higher."

"What else is there? If I'm not going up, I'm either going down or staying stagnant."

Kurt studied him. "Where is this coming from?"

"I spent years moving up. Now I just take out target after target, and train assassins once they're out of the newbie phase." Brad finally allowed his yawn to come through.

"You get the best assignments. You've worked from home and I personally paid for your wife's in-home salon. What more could you want? You even get to go to Italy."

Brad scooted his chair closer to the desk. "Faye's salon was a bribe — to get me to pretend there isn't a glass ceiling here at the knife shop."

"Just say it."

"What?"

"Neither of us are idiots. The subtext of every conversation we've had since you returned from jail has been a screaming neon light. When are you going to tell me what you really want?"

"I want to move up in the company."

Kurt rose and pressed his palms on the desk. "You want my job. Admit it."

Brad laughed at the absurdity of the idea.

"You're laughing at me?" he exclaimed.

"Why would I gun for *your* job? You're the boss's son. Am I going to seek an adoption from Ralf?"

Kurt sat back down. "You can't get much higher up, Morris."

Brad considered where to go with that statement. The conversation could go in so many directions at this point.

"Your silence isn't reassuring."

"I have no plans to take your position."

"What, then?"

"You have assassins who don't have to show up here every day and sell knives to housewives and boy scouts. Nobody sees them, but they get things done. You act like there isn't some sort of inner circle, but we both know better. I want in. There's no reason you shouldn't trust me to be part of that. The company wouldn't be what it is today without me."

"*That's* what all this is about?" Kurt looked at Brad, assessing him for too long.

Brad had the impression that he'd actually managed to surprise his boss. Or was he faking, to keep Brad off guard? Maybe he *hadn't* realized that Brad had discovered the truth and was plotting revenge. Maybe he'd seen him as merely ambitious this entire time.

Brad tried to keep his tone casual. "Scott's injured. Why not let me give his position a whirl? See how it goes."

"What about when he returns?" Kurt twirled a pencil as if bored, but the intensity in his eyes showed his irritation.

"*Is* he returning?"

"Yes."

Brad stared in silence, doing his best to look skeptical.

"Look, even if I wanted to give you the opportunity, it isn't my call."

"Need Daddy's permission?"

His boss's face reddened. "This discussion is over. I brought you in here to discuss your daughter's visit to the precinct."

Back to that. Brad took a deep breath. "It sounds like you know all about that already."

"I wouldn't say *all* about it."

Brad considered his wording. "It was nothing."

"Nothing? Really? No suspicions about a missing kid?"

Kurt did know. But why wouldn't he? He made it his business to know all the things.

"Why were the police questioning your daughter about it?"

Brad readjusted his weight in the seat. "There was some question due to her having been the last one to speak with him at school that day."

"Wasn't it more of an argument?"

"Not really." Brad's mind raced to find a new topic. If he was more rested and less stressed, it wouldn't have been a problem.

"That was what I heard." The other side of Kurt's mouth curved up.

Brad wanted to punch him in that mouth. "If you have a question, why don't you ask?"

"Is your daughter something we need to worry about?"

"No, she isn't *someone* you have to worry about. The fact that she was only questioned for a short while should assure you of that much."

Kurt smirked, clearly enjoying the exchange for some reason. "What's her involvement with that missing kid?"

"Does it matter?"

"If it could impact the company, you'd better believe it."

"It isn't going to."

"Fill me in on the details, regardless. You never know when surprises might surface. I don't like being taken off guard."

Brad held back a smile as he answered the question. "Hadley and Nate didn't have a close relationship. They were friends because their moms were close before Allison's death, nothing more than that. It wasn't like the kids had any sort of deep friendship. They'd both experienced loss, and they had a bit of a connection over that. Nothing major."

Kurt's eyes lit up. "Didn't?"

"What?"

"You said the kids *didn't* have a close relationship.

Makes it sound like the kid is dead. Do you know something I don't?"

Brad's heart skipped a beat. That was a small but important slip, and he couldn't afford another one.

"Is he dead?" A slow smile spread across Kurt's face.

"How would I know?" Brad kept his tone even. "All I meant is that Hadley wasn't close to Nate before his disappearance. She was one of the popular kids, and he wasn't. It was coincidence that she was the last one to speak with him before he ran off."

Kurt leaned forward. "Is there anything you need help with?"

"Such as?"

"You tell me."

"No. Thanks."

Silence lingered before Kurt spoke. "How's she doing? You know, since her *friend* is missing."

"She feels just as bad as she would if any of her classmates disappeared."

"Did you kill him?"

"No."

"You sure?"

Brad snorted. "I'd know if I killed someone."

"Do you know what happened to the missing kid?"

"He's missing." Time to go on the offensive. "How's Ralf?"

"My dad?" Kurt jolted slightly at the change of subject.

Good.

Brad leaned forward. "Ralf. How is he?"

"Why are you asking about him?"

"I keep running into him. Something isn't wrong, is it?"

"No." Kurt squared his shoulders. "He's fine. Not that it's any of your business."

STACY CLAFLIN & NOLON KING

"My dad was a serious working man, and he always told me how important it was to stay in the know with whatever business I ended up in. That was good advice, don't you think?"

"What are you saying?"

"What do you *think* I'm saying?"

"I hope you're saying that you want to be a good employee so you can possibly move up in the organization."

"I've been with the company for much longer than most," Brad said. "I want more responsibility, more trust, and more freedom. That isn't much to ask as someone who has done so much for BlueBlade."

"Take out your target, then we'll talk."

Brad decided not to push his luck, now that he'd gotten what he wanted — Kurt off-balance, and possibly open to discussion. His heart pounded as Kurt showed him out of the office.

He was significantly closer to getting what he needed from his boss.

But in order to do that, Brad would have to defy the agent's orders not to kill his target.

Chapter Twenty-Five

HADLEY CHECKED her mirror once more before grabbing her purse. She wasn't sure what she needed for her job at the car wash. It wasn't like she'd interviewed and gotten to ask any questions. Or that she'd even wanted the gig.

But here she was. Punching her ticket to freedom.

Hopefully, she'd figure it out once she got there.

Her heart pounded just thinking about it. Did the boss know she was coming? Why had he been so willing to hire her sight unseen? Was he also a spy?

She made her way downstairs, waving to Mom through the window to her salon.

Mom paused in giving some lady a haircut and waved back. Mouthed, "Good luck. Call me!"

Hadley nodded and made her way to her car. There was an unfamiliar car parked behind it.

Her breath hitched. Was someone waiting for her? To accuse her of killing Nate?

The agent emerged from the car and hurried over, her heels clacking with each step.

Relief washed through her. "Is everything okay?"

"I want to go over a few details before you start work."

Hadley checked the time. "It'll only take a minute, right?"

"Yes, nothing to worry about. If you're a few minutes late, I'll give them the heads up."

"This is actually my first job. I've always been too busy with my plays for work."

The agent — Hadley tried to remember her name — tightened her long, dark ponytail. "And that's why you're perfect for this."

Hadley tilted her head. "I am?"

"Yes. Feel free to make liberal newbie mistakes and talk openly about your lack of experience. The less they expect you to be up to something, the better."

"What exactly am I up to? I know I'm supposed to listen for any suspicious conversations. But what does that mean?"

Squeal! Hiss!

A school bus stopped across the street.

Kids from school piled out, laughing and joking.

Hadley's face warmed. She should've left earlier. Now, they would not only notice she hadn't been at school, but that she was talking to the agent — who looked every bit like one on TV.

They'd think she was guiltier now more than ever.

She turned away, hoping nobody would see her.

A girl called her name.

Hadley pretended not to hear it.

Someone else hollered something about Nate.

Tears stung her eyes. She'd left school to get away from all of that, but there was no escaping it. Would she have to put up with more at the job?

"Do you want me to talk to them?" asked the agent.

"No. Just tell me what I need to do, so I can get out of here."

"If you're sure."

Hadley nodded.

"Okay, back to the car wash. Make mistakes, be unassuming, listen in on conversations, and go through any paperwork you can find."

"That's it? No breaking into safes or anything? Putting trackers on cars? Installing bugs?"

The agent shook her head. "Like you said, you don't have any training. I just need some ears and eyes on the inside. If you can befriend any of the higher ups, all the better. If somebody gives you info outright, that'll be golden."

"What if I don't find anything?"

"Then you'll try again tomorrow." She reached into her jacket. "Do you still have my card?"

"Yeah, and I put your number in my phone."

"Good. Call me if you run into trouble."

Hadley's stomach knotted. "Do you think I will?"

"No. They hire a lot of entry-level workers. They won't suspect anything, unless you give them a reason to."

"What if someone asks me about Nate? Seems like the whole town thinks I had something to do with his disappearance."

"Tell them you think he ran away, or whatever you feel comfortable with. The more natural you are, the more likely they'll believe you."

Hadley twisted some hair around her finger. "I hope I can remember all of this."

The agent put her hand on Hadley's shoulder. "You'll do fine. Just remember you're there to listen — that's the only thing you need to worry about. Can you do that?"

"Yeah."

"Good. Give me an update after your shift."

Hadley sighed. "Okay. Don't be mad if I forget. This is a lot to remember."

"I'll be in touch if I don't hear from you."

Then she got back into her car and drove off.

At least all the kids were gone. She didn't have to deal with them.

The drive to the car wash went too quickly. Her mouth dried as she stared at the building from the parking spot. She didn't even know who she was supposed to talk to once she got in.

There was only one way to find out.

She stood tall, gripped her purse, and marched toward the building like she owned the place.

So much for being bumbling and unassuming. But that wasn't her. If she was going to do a good job, she needed to play to her strengths.

She flung open the door with flair and took in the sight. A lot of shelves with car supplies — sponges, towels, soaps, and whatnot. A large counter with a trio of registers. Windows that showed the cars going through the wash.

A guy who looked like Napoleon Dynamite came around the corner. "Can I help you?"

She held out her hand. "I'm Hadley. I work here now."

"You're the new girl? Wow, okay. Spencer said you were starting. Have you ever worked a till before?"

"You mean the registers?"

"Right."

"No, but it can't be that hard. Can it?"

"When you're first learning, you'd better believe it."

"Great."

"What about the emergency protocols? Did Spencer go over any of that with you?"

"Emergencies? Like what?"

He frowned. "Seriously?"

"Yeah."

Napoleon motioned toward the car wash. "Things get stuck. And we have rules for theft. Stuff like that."

"Rules for theft? They allow stealing?"

"No." He sounded super annoyed. "Rules for how to *handle* thieves. What would you do if you saw someone leaving with a bottle of car wash?"

"Ask them to put it back?" Hadley answered with a shrug.

"This is going to be a long afternoon."

She sighed.

It sure was.

Chapter Twenty-Six

BRAD SLAMMED HIS LOCKER SHUT, eager to get home. Ever since his earlier conversation with Kurt, his boss had been testing him. He'd had Brad doing janitorial work, doing a supply run, and answering phones — all things reserved for the lowest-level employees. Ones who didn't even know about the assassination side of things.

But Brad had managed to do all of the menial work with a grin. It pissed off his boss, thus achieving the desired result. If Kurt wanted to see what he would do to move up in the company, Brad would do it with gusto.

With any luck, all of this would soon be behind him. The Bergmanns would be in prison for life — not that it would be a long time for Ralf — and Brad would be able to find a new career.

He didn't even know what he wanted to pursue, but the sky was the limit.

Brad slid on his jacket and headed for the back door.

Kurt appeared from his office, his face red.

"Everything okay, boss?"

"Get in here!" Kurt bellowed.

"If this is about the toilet, Roger went after I cleaned it, so you can't blame me for what he left behind."

"Now!" Spittle flew from Kurt's mouth.

Brad stepped inside. "Is there a problem?"

"Do you think?" Kurt slammed the door and gestured for Brad to sit.

He did.

Kurt did not. "What were you *thinking*?"

"About what, exactly?"

"Don't play coy with me!"

"I'm not playing. What are you talking about?"

Kurt paced, flailing his arms like an injured bird. "You know exactly what this is about!"

"If it isn't the toilet, then no, I actually don't."

"The Slippery Fish!"

"What about it? I haven't gone near it, as requested."

Kurt's nostrils flared. "Your daughter is working there! Did you think I wouldn't find out?"

It all made sense now. Brad had all but forgotten about Hadley's job, he'd been so busy proving himself to Kurt.

"What do you have to say for yourself?"

"I had nothing to do with that."

"Sure you didn't! You've been jonesing that place for weeks."

"I went there once." He couldn't prove more than that. "And I haven't been there since then."

"It was more than once!"

"Was it?"

He stopped pacing and stared Brad down. "You need to make her quit!"

"Is she doing something wrong?"

"Other than spying for you?" Kurt shouted.

Brad didn't look away. "Her job has nothing to do with me. And really, don't you think if I was going to send in a spy, I would choose someone more inconspicuous than my *daughter*?"

"Why is she there?"

He shrugged.

"You have to give me more than that!"

"I. Don't. Know. She didn't ask my opinion on the matter. I'd imagine now that she's doing virtual school, she's looking for something else to do. I guess she wants a job. She used to stay busy with her school plays."

"And your neighbor."

Brad jumped up and clenched his fists. Held back from punching his boss.

Needed to stay in control for a little longer. Soon, he'd be behind bars.

Couldn't let him get under his skin.

Kurt's brows furrowed. "Let me speak in a way that will get through your thick, ugly skull — make her quit, or you can forget about moving up in the company! The only thing you'll be doing is cleaning the toilets with a toothbrush after Roger has his way with them."

"You think she'll listen to me? My daughter has always done exactly what she wants."

"Then convince her, just like I'm convincing you."

"I'm not going to threaten my child."

"Too bad for you."

"Her job was not my idea!"

"Doesn't matter. Make her quit."

"You clearly don't have a teenager."

"For good reason. I knew it would cloud my judgment, which is needed in this business."

Brad bit his tongue. He needed to come up with a compromise, and quick. Something to shut Kurt up, at least for now.

"Nothing to say for yourself?"

Brad snapped his attention back to his boss. "Why don't we use this to our advantage?"

"What are you talking about?"

"She could report to me anything she finds that could be useful to *our* organization."

Kurt hesitated. "How would that work? She doesn't know what would help us. She doesn't even know you're an assassin."

"Obviously. But she can still tell me anything weird. I don't even have to mention your involvement. Think about it. Inside information on the other assassination ring. This could be priceless."

Kurt started to say something, but then stopped.

"What?"

"Stop being ridiculous and follow orders. Get her to quit, or you're going to be cleaning toilets for the rest of your career."

"You'd really waste my talent on janitorial work?"

"When you're a loose cannon, yes! Get out of here, and figure out how you're going to force your daughter's hand."

"But the—"

"I said, go!"

"You—"

"Now!"

"I haven't done anything wrong. In fact, I've been more than generous by putting up with all the petty work you've thrown at me today. You need to hear me."

"I don't have to do anything. Get out!"

Brad didn't budge.

"Am I speaking too quietly?"

"You should know I'm no pushover."

"So, that's the way it's going to be." Kurt stormed toward his desk.

Not the door.

Brad opened his mouth to say something, but stopped cold before he could say anything.

Kurt aimed a pistol at him.

Brad didn't give his boss a chance to use it.

Instead he fled from the office, slamming the door behind him.

Chapter Twenty-Seven

BRAD CALLED Agent Bancroft as he sped away from the knife shop. His heart felt like it would explode out of his chest.

Kurt had pulled a gun on him.

Brad had no doubt that it had been loaded.

"Kurt found out about Hadley's job." Brad gasped for air and sped through a light as it turned red.

"I take it he wasn't happy."

"He pulled a gun on me!"

"What?"

"Everything was going great. I had him convinced I wanted nothing more than to move up in the company. He insisted that I focus on killing Giuliano Franco, but he was testing my loyalty."

"And then he heard that Hadley—?"

"Yes!" He took a sharp corner, looking behind him.

Nobody was following him, but he wasn't taking any chances.

"Okay, calm down. I'll find a way to make it look like you took Franco out."

"What about Hadley's job?"

"It's going to take some finagling to make Giuliano Franco look dead. For now, we'll have to hope Kurt will change his mind about Hadley after you manage to kill your target."

"In Italy? Without him setting up my travels?"

"I know a guy. You can tell Bergmann that *you* know him, that he owes you. It'll make you look even more serious, like a real go-getter."

Brad stifled an eyeroll and pulled into a small alley, parking between two dumpsters. "You didn't see how furious he was about the car wash."

"I can imagine."

"Then get my daughter out of there. I don't want her involved anymore."

"First, Giuliano Franco."

"No! My daughter's safety is the immediate concern."

"You need to give me at least twenty minutes to reach my guy in Italy and discuss this. We can fake Franco's death."

"Kurt will know I didn't do it, unless he thinks I've been saving up for a supersonic jet."

"You can tell him you called in a favor and had it done immediately, since you knew how important it was."

"Or he's going to think I'm trying to piss him off by subcontracting the job to someone he doesn't know. At best, that's poor judgment creating a possible security breach. At worst, it makes me look like I'm getting ready to go rogue. That I've been building a competing organization behind his back."

"It's your job to make him think it's a good idea."

"None of this stops him from going after Hadley. Get her out of there so I know she's safe, then I'll go back to Kurt."

"Look, Morris. You need to chill out and listen to me. I'm trying to save your bacon."

"I'll get her myself! Do you hear me? I'll drag her out. That actually works to my advantage, because word will get back to the Bergmanns that I've followed Kurt's orders. We'll both be safe."

"Her shift is almost over! Let her finish, or I might have to alter the terms of our arrangement."

Bancroft hung up before he could respond.

Insanity.

He pulled out of the alley and headed for the car wash.

Chapter Twenty-Eight

HADLEY WIPED hair from her forehead as she climbed into her car. Every muscle in her body ached. There was *so* much to remember. She'd been so busy trying to learn the till and the emergency procedures that she'd had no time to look for anything the agent wanted her to look for.

She was sure nobody she'd met that day had anything to do with assassinations.

The afternoon had been a colossal failure.

What was she supposed to say to the agent? That all she'd learned was how to ungunk the soap sprayers and how to give refunds to dissatisfied customers?

If she couldn't find anything helpful for Agent Bancroft, she'd give birth to Duke's baby in prison. Assuming she managed to stay alive until the birth.

She swung by a coffee stand and got a raspberry latte to settle her nerves. Hopefully that would help her get through the rest of the night. She still had homework to do, for virtual school.

The caffeine gave her a slight buzz as she sipped it. If she didn't have the baby to think about, she'd have gotten a double or triple shot. But now she had to be more responsible.

Hadley stopped at a light and took another long sip. If nothing else, the warmth of the drink was comforting after such a tiring afternoon.

She noticed a black Land Rover in the rearview. Her heart sank. Duke's had been similar. Whenever she saw one like this, it made her think of him.

The light turned green, and she put the latte in the cupholder. She tried to think of anything suspicious at the car wash — anything she could report to the agent if she called.

Two stoplights later, she noticed the same vehicle behind her. There weren't many of those in Pine Harbor — so few that Duke always waved to the other drivers when he saw them — so it had to be the same one.

Just before turning to her neighborhood, she saw the Land Rover was still back there.

It felt like stepping back in time to the night of Nate's death. When he'd followed her.

If she'd learned anything from that night, it was that getting out was what got her into trouble. And parking outside the house left too much room. By the time she got out and ran to the house, the other person would have plenty of time to leap out and grab her.

Why had she stopped carrying a knife?

Because it had led to her killing her friend.

Now she was defenseless.

Instead of turning into the neighborhood, she kept going. Watched the rearview mirror from the corner of her eye.

Every time she turned, so did the Land Rover.

Her hands shook.

What was she supposed to do?

Dad would know. But she'd have to call him first. She couldn't reach her purse on the passenger seat while driving.

Each light was green. Why couldn't she get a yellow or red light now that she wanted one? Whenever she was late for school, she always got them.

After about five green lights in a row, she finally got a yellow. She could've easily made it, but she slowed.

The Land Rover was behind her. Still.

There had to be a way she could lose him.

She reached over to the passenger seat without being obvious. What if the guy had a gun? She didn't want him shooting at her, thinking she might be grabbing one of her own.

Her fingers barely reached the purse. She stretched more.

Honk!

Green light.

She sat up and hit the gas. Next time, she'd have to be less subtle and just grab the purse. Dad would drop everything and help her. Maybe call some of his assassin friends, too. They could gang up on the Land Rover.

Hadley took the next turn, even though it didn't really lead anywhere. Just to some rundown apartments and a creepy gas station beyond that. At least the road let out to another main road eventually.

The vehicle turned.

Her breath hitched. If there had been any doubts before, they were squelched now.

She was definitely being followed.

What did the guy want? Was it someone from the car wash who was onto her? That wouldn't be too surprising. Assassins weren't stupid, and it wouldn't be hard for them to figure out that she was the daughter of another trained killer.

When she stopped to let a lady with a three-legged dog cross the road, Hadley leaned over quickly and grabbed her cell out of her purse. Held it in her lap as she called her dad.

The light from the screen was too bright — the other driver could probably see its reflection on her face.

Dad's phone went to voicemail.

What was he doing that was so important he couldn't answer her call?

Maybe she should call the agent. Even if she was mad about Hadley not making any progress at the car wash, she could at least tell her how to handle being followed. Maybe she'd even come and help.

Honk!

Hadley looked up and hit the gas.

Now the Land Rover was on her tail. It would hit her if the driver pushed the gas much harder.

Her mouth dried. She sped up.

So did the other vehicle.

Still right behind her.

Then it bumped her.

Chapter Twenty-Nine

BRAD TURNED down the street of the car wash. Slowed as he approached, checking the parking lot for Hadley's car.

It wasn't there. She must've already left for the day.

Relief washed through him. She was fine. Possibly even home already.

Unless someone had taken her away against her will.

But if that were the case, would they take her car?

Maybe. They could've had it towed. Or hidden in the back seat and waited for Hadley to get in.

Maybe his little girl was driving to some remote location at gunpoint, so that Kurt could bury her after he executed her.

Brad's heart hammered.

He grabbed his phone to call Hadley when it rang in his hand.

The agent.

He wanted to curse her out. But she was their only way out of all of this.

"What?" he answered.

"I told you to go to work. What are you doing at the car wash?"

"You tracking me?"

"I told you that I have people watching. Look, I've—"

"Where is Hadley?" he demanded. "She's not at work."

"She was supposed to call me, but hasn't yet."

"She's in trouble — Kurt got to her!"

"His car hasn't budged, unlike yours."

"Just because he personally didn't abduct her doesn't mean he didn't send someone to do the dirty work."

"Brad, you need to listen to me. Hadley is probably on her way home, planning to call me from there."

"You don't know exactly where she is? Aren't you tracking her, too?"

"Go back to BlueBlade before Kurt leaves."

"Are you tracking my daughter's car?" he demanded.

"Someone removed the tracker."

Brad swore and hung up. Drove around the parking lot to see if Hadley's car was anywhere in sight.

It wasn't.

He headed back to the knife shop, ignoring Agent Bancroft's repeated calls. He'd talk to her once his daughter was safe.

Kurt's car was still there.

He had half a mind to pull a gun on *him*.

After parking, Brad retrieved the emergency Glock he kept in a secret compartment in the trunk of his car and slid one into his inner jacket pocket, then put a knife in his back pants pocket.

Now he was ready to face off with his boss. It didn't matter that the agent wanted Kurt alive. If Faye had to smuggle Hadley out of the country while Brad rotted in prison for the rest of his life, so be it. At least his daughter would still be alive.

He marched inside and pounded on Kurt's door.

"I'm busy," his boss called.

"Not too busy for this!" Brad continued knocking.

"You dare show up again?"

"You'd better believe it. Open up!"

No response.

"Giuliano Franco is dead."

A beat of silence, then the door flung open. Kurt stared at Brad, face red and hair disheveled. "What did you say?"

"Where's my daughter?"

"How the hell would I know?"

"Less than an hour ago, you were waving a pistol in my face and threatening her life. Ring any bells?"

Kurt grabbed his arm, yanked him inside, and slammed the door shut. "What did you say about Franco?"

"We can talk about him after you tell me where Hadley is."

"*You* were supposed to make her quit. If she's missing, not my concern. But if you want me to help you look for her, you'd better explain what's going on with your target."

"He's dead. Not a lot else to explain."

"There's no way the bastard is dead. He's in Italy, so there's no way you could've killed him. What are you trying to pull?"

Brad sat at the desk and kicked his feet up. "Look into it, the deed is done. Time for me to move up in the company. Who else could've accomplished the task so quickly? No one, that's who."

"You're crazy!" Kurt shoved Brad's feet off his desk. "Franco can't be dead. That's impossible!"

Brad lifted a brow. "Is it?"

"Yes!"

"Are you worried because you didn't *really* want him dead?"

Kurt's nostrils flared.

"Kind of like how you didn't actually want my last target dead, right? The truth is, *I* was the intended target."

"You're insane."

"Call your people. They'll confirm that I'm telling the truth."

Swearing profusely, Kurt went to his side of the desk and picked up his cell. Swiped his fingers across the screen. His expression tightened. Then he brought the phone closer to his face. "Call Ché Poli."

Hopefully Bancroft had come through on her plan to make his target look dead. Otherwise, he was going to have a real problem.

Kurt turned around and spoke softer — as if Brad still couldn't hear him.

With his boss distracted, Brad took out his phone to text his daughter.

A slew of missed calls and texts.

It was a relief that she was alive, but she had to be in trouble if she'd attempted to reach him so many times. He clicked over to read the texts. They were short, but the message was clear.

Someone was chasing her in the car.

Kurt had sent someone to scare her.

And that better be the only thing he'd sent the person to do.

His boss turned around, his face drained of color. "Franco's actually dead."

"Of course he is — you told me to kill him." Brad leaped up, barely able to control his fury. "Who did you send to tail my daughter?"

"What are you talking about?"

Brad grabbed Kurt's collar. "Don't play stupid with me. Where is Hadley?"

"You had Franco killed."

"I know people. Who did you send after my daughter?"

Kurt shoved Brad against the desk, knocking a few things to the floor in the process. "I told you to stay away from the Slippery Fish, but you didn't listen."

Brad swung at Kurt, but his boss blocked the shot. "You should've known better than to underestimate me — especially when it comes to my family."

Kurt reached into his pocket, but Brad pulled his arm away.

"Where is Hadley?"

"I don't know. Sal hasn't gotten back to me."

Brad punched him square in the jaw.

Chapter Thirty

THE VEHICLE RAMMED Hadley's car again, this time harder.

He wanted her to know it was on purpose.

She was his target. Just like the people Dad went after.

Hadley squeezed the steering wheel and pressed the gas as hard as she could, hitting her head against the headrest in the process.

The car behind her sped up, too.

No place to turn, nowhere to hide.

It was coming faster than she was driving.

She floored it, hoping a police cruiser would show up.

Her heart hammered, blood rushed in her ears.

Some kids were jaywalking ahead. Slowly.

Hadley blared her horn.

They didn't pay her any attention.

She was almost on them.

One turned to her, wide-eyed. Said something to the others.

They ran.

But not fast enough.

Hadley cranked the steering wheel. Jolted as the front wheel hit the curb.

Missed the kids.

The car behind her bumped her.

She screamed. Hit the gas. Readjusted the wheel.

Thud!

Her hands shook as she tried to simultaneously go faster and stay in her lane.

Then decided to swerve.

A car in the other lane. Heading straight for her.

Honk!

She whipped the car back into the right lane.

The Land Rover was right beside her.

Metal on metal as the side of her car scraped against it.

Hadley could see the other driver.

His weathered face glowered at her. He made an obscene gesture.

She pressed the gas.

The Rover sped up, too.

The oncoming car honked.

Hadley slammed on the brakes.

Nearly hit the steering wheel. Barely had time to turn it.

The oncoming car whizzed by.

She gasped for air.

The Land Rover skidded to a stop. Left a trail of rubber on the road. Turned.

It was coming after her head-on.

Tears stung her eyes.

She had to do something. Couldn't run.

Probably couldn't get away while on this road.

Two options. Either turn around and flee, or try to avoid the Rover as it aimed for her.

No time to think. Just to act.

Hadley pressed the gas as hard as she could. Jerked forward. Turned the wheel. Ran over the sidewalk.

Kept going, half on and half off.

Passed the vehicle.

Its tires squealed as it turned again.

Her car bumped as she pulled off the sidewalk.

Bang!

She screamed. Had one of her tires blown out?

Bang!

A bullet flew into the speed limit sign in front of her.

He was shooting at her.

The man had a gun.

She was going to die.

She struggled to keep the car going straight.

Prayed that someone would call the cops. People living in the apartments wouldn't ignore the gunfire.

Hopefully.

In the rearview mirror, the other car was almost fully turned around.

She was almost to the intersection.

Hadley pressed the gas. Glanced back and forth between the road ahead and the vehicle behind.

Both were approaching too quickly.

Ahead, cars flew through the busy road. Behind, the Rover gained speed.

Bang!

Her breath hitched.

If she survived this, she would never leave the safety of her home again.

The traffic light ahead was red.

Still red.

If she stopped, the larger vehicle would ram into her again.

The light turned green.

Green.

Her legs and arms went weak with relief.

She managed to find the strength to both hold on and press forward.

Shot through the intersection at twice the legal speed. That would catch someone's attention.

The other car raced through even faster, gaining on her.

There was a small break in the oncoming cars. She'd barely have enough room to make the left-hand turn.

If she timed it right.

If the Land Rover didn't smash into her first.

Hadley held her breath and released her foot from the gas pedal.

The break between the cars approached.

So did the man who wanted her dead.

Her palms moistened as she figured out the timing.

Now.

She spun the wheel, her hands sliding. Dug her nails in.

Turned. Seemingly in slow motion.

The break in cars narrowed as the car up ahead closed the distanced. Blared the horn.

Hadley hit the gas.

The wheels spun.

Her car turned, went in a circle.

She pressed the brakes.

The screeching of metal on metal.

Hadley braced herself for the impact.

Realized the Rover had crashed into the oncoming traffic.

More metal twisted.

Her car's tires squealed as she skidded to a stop. Barely missed a minivan.

Bang!

She whipped her head in the direction of the shot.

The weathered man now stumbled toward her car, bloody and limping. Gun aimed at her.

Her bladder gave out.

She ducked.

Bang!

Glass shattered as the window next to her exploded.

The passenger side window cracked, but didn't fall apart.

Shards of glass stuck to her, some digging into skin.

Hadley crawled to the passenger side, staying low. Fought with the handle.

Shoved open the door.

Climbed out. Cowered beside the wheel.

Bang!

Hiss.

The car's weight shifted as the tire on the other side went flat.

Hands grasped her shoulders. Pulled her back.

Hadley screamed and flailed.

"I'm here to help!"

She stopped yelling, turned to the voice.

It belonged to a guy about Duke's age. He kind of reminded her of him. His eyes were just as caring.

"Come with me." He led her inside a shop.

More gunfire rang out. Shouts. Squealing breaks. Metal on metal.

Then blue-and-red lights shone on the street.

"Were you shot?"

She turned to him. Followed his gaze.

Her pants were covered in blood.

It wasn't her bladder that had given out.

The baby was in danger.

She collapsed into the stranger's arms and sobbed.

Chapter Thirty-One

BRAD HELD Kurt against the wall. "Where is Hadley?"

His boss spit in his face. "Like I said, Sal hasn't gotten back to me."

"That isn't good enough!"

Kurt squirmed out of the hold and shoved Brad. "He's not going to kill her. Just rough her up enough to scare her from going anywhere near the Slippery Fish again."

"That makes everything okay, then!" Brad lunged for him.

Kurt darted out of the way and ran for his desk.

Where he kept his pistol. And probably other weapons.

Brad slammed into him, knocking them both to the floor.

Kurt reached for his throat. "You're going to pay for killing Franco!"

Brad wrapped his hands around Kurt's wrists and struggled to free himself. "You *told* me to kill him. That was my job!"

"You already knew it was a setup." Kurt grabbed his

hair and slammed the back of Brad's head against the floor.

Brad kicked him, leaped up, and pinned his boss down. "Why would that be?"

"You keep looking into things you have no business knowing about."

"Like the car wash?"

Brad dug his knee into Kurt's stomach. His boss struggled for air and used his leg to flip Brad off of him. "Exactly."

Brad slammed into the desk. "You're never going to kill me."

"That's what you think."

"How many times have you tried to take my life?"

Kurt glared at him, jumped up, and headed for his desk.

Brad wrapped his feet around his boss's ankles.

He went down, crashing with a loud thud. "You're more trouble than you're worth."

Brad squeezed Kurt's neck. "I'll happily walk away."

"We don't leave loose threads," he choked out.

"Is that why you killed my dad?" Brad shouted. "Was he too big a threat for you?"

Kurt's eyes widened.

"Didn't think I knew about that?" Brad squeezed harder. "I know everything, except why you did it. *Why?*"

Kurt pulled on Brad's hands. "Can't ... talk."

Brad loosened his grip slightly. "Why did you kill my dad?"

"Let ... go."

It was a risk. Kurt might not talk either way.

But he needed to take the chance. Needed answers.

Brad let go.

Kurt coughed and sat up.

"Spill it!"

He scooted back.

"Don't try anything!" Brad pulled out his gun. Aimed it at his boss. "Tell me everything. Were you jealous? He was going places — we all know that."

Kurt held out his palms. "Put that down."

Brad waved it around. "Talk! Now."

"Only if you set that down." He gestured toward the desk.

"You don't call the shots right now."

Kurt inched toward the desk.

"Talk, or I shoot."

"Okay. Calm down."

Brad hit him in the side of the head with the weapon. "This is your last warning before your father has to clean your brains from the walls."

Kurt laughed.

Laughed.

The room took on a red hue.

"You think this is funny?"

Kurt shoved him. "You have it all wrong, Morris."

"What are you talking about?" Brad pressed the gun against his temple.

"I didn't kill John because I wanted him dead. Idiot."

The weapon shook in Brad's hand. "What do you mean?"

"If I wanted to move up in the business, I needed to do it. Father's orders, no questions asked. I actually kind of liked your dad." Kurt shrugged. "But it was what it was. Taking over the family business has been my lifelong dream. I wasn't going to refuse the opportunity."

Brad stepped back. "Ralf put a hit on him?"

Kurt rubbed his temple. "Exactly."

"Why?"

"Wasn't my place to ask questions."

Brad pressed the gun to his chest. "Bull! Why did he put out the hit?"

Kurt sighed dramatically. "John — like *you* — wouldn't leave well enough alone. Was told to stop looking into things, but wouldn't. Like father, like son. Don't ask me what the details were. I honestly don't know. Wasn't given that information, and it's since been destroyed."

Brad took a deep breath, taking in the news.

Ralf was behind Dad's death. Kurt had pulled the trigger, but it wouldn't have happened if Ralf hadn't demanded it.

Kurt stepped away from Brad.

"Don't move!"

"You still gonna kill me?" Kurt tilted his head, the corners of his mouth wavering.

"Do you think this is *funny*?"

"Kind of. How long did it take you to figure out it was an inside job? You joined this business to get revenge. Yet you ended up working for the very people you wanted to kill."

Click.

Brad readied the gun. Didn't care about his promise to let the monster live.

He was going to pay for what he'd done.

Brad took a step closer.

The door burst open.

"Put that gun down!" Agent Bancroft's voice rang out. "I need him alive."

Kurt's mouth fell open. "June?"

Brad stepped to the side and looked back and forth between them. "You two know each other?"

The agent's expression tightened. "I only came to you after I failed to get close enough to him."

Kurt appeared just as taken aback. "How … I mean, who are you? Really?"

"CIA."

Kurt swore. "I should've seen that coming. It all makes sense now."

"Not to me," Brad said. "What's going on?"

Bancroft stepped between them. Moved Brad's arm so the gun was no longer pointed at Kurt. She whipped out handcuffs and restrained him. "I'm taking you in for attempted murder."

"Of who?" Kurt demanded.

"Brad here."

"He had the gun on me!"

"That isn't what I saw." She turned to Brad. "He had a gun on you."

"He did earlier."

Kurt spat on him.

Bancroft yanked him toward the door, but stopped and turned to Brad. "You're going to the hospital."

"I'm not hurt."

"I just got word that Hadley was admitted."

"What?"

"Just get down there."

Brad turned to Kurt. "All of this because she got a part-time job at the car wash?"

"What do you think? And by the way, I lied about telling Sal not to kill her."

Brad aimed the gun at him.

The agent shook her head at him, and tugged Kurt out of the office.

Brad bolted for his car.

Chapter Thirty-Two

A FEW WEEKS LATER ...

BRAD WRAPPED his arm around Faye as they approached the front desk.

She sniffled, keeping her head low.

He made eye contact with the heavyset guy behind the counter. His name was Clint. Or maybe Coby. "We're here to visit Hadley Morris."

"I'll see if she's available." He typed on the keyboard, leaning closer to the computer screen.

"Dr. Fallow said this would be a good time. I just got off the phone with him."

Faye nestled closer against Brad.

Clint — Brad checked his name tag — glanced up at him. "I'm sorry, Mr. Morris. Hadley needed to be sedated about ten minutes ago. She won't be awake for some time."

Faye gasped.

Brad rubbed circles on her back. "Are you sure?"

"Yeah. Says so right here." Clint pointed to the screen as if Brad could see it.

"Can we at least see her?" Faye asked.

"I'll have to check with Dr. Fallow. Have a seat." Clint motioned toward the waiting area.

"We're her parents," Faye snapped.

"Sorry, but rules are rules."

Brad guided Faye toward the chairs. "I'm sure the doctor will let us see her."

"What if he doesn't?"

"Then we'll call Dr. Trellis and see if she can help out. Since they've been working closely on Hadley's case, she has some pull."

Brad helped her into a chair and kissed her cheek. "We'll see her today, even if we have to wait until she wakes up."

Faye sighed. "Why do you think they had to sedate her?"

If it was anything like the last time, she'd probably attacked a nurse. Dr. Fallow had called them after the incident.

Brad kept that thought to himself. "Maybe she just needed a rest."

Faye gave him a look that said she didn't believe him.

His phone beeped with a text.

"You going to check that?"

"It's probably just the agent again."

"Does she want to destroy our lives even more?"

"Neither Hadley nor I are going to jail."

Faye scowled. "But Hadley's still locked up."

"Only until she faces her grief."

"Don't you worry she'll confess to …" Faye looked around the empty waiting room. "You know. What she did."

"She knows better."

"But she isn't in her right mind." Faye clung to him. "What if the only thing that will clear her conscience is to admit what happened?"

"She'll be okay. She's strong."

"I don't know if anyone's that strong." After a moment of silence, Faye added, "I think I was starting to look forward to being a grandmother."

Brad's phone beeped again.

"Maybe you should get that."

Brad didn't want to think about the agent, or anything involving her.

She'd changed the terms of their deal after Kurt's arrest.

Now Brad was supposed to return to BlueBlade, where Ralf was back in charge.

Kurt hadn't given up any information after Bancroft took him.

It was Brad's job to get her the information she wanted, no matter the consequences.

The agent didn't know that Brad was going to kill Ralf.

The Series Continues...

Brad and his family still aren't in the clear. What to know what happens next? The story continues in *Dead For Life*, *Dead For Good Book 5*.

Pick up your copy of Dead For Life today!

A Quick Favor...

If you enjoyed this book, please take a moment to write a short review on your favorite online bookstore so other readers can enjoy it, too.

Thanks so much!

About the Authors

Stacy Claflin is a USA Today bestselling thriller author who has published more than 75 novels, including Girl in Trouble and The Perfect Death. She has always been curious about the human mind, and in her quest to learn more, she earned a degree in Psychology. Her favorite course was Abnormal Behavior, which has been useful in writing fiction.

Her love for thrillers goes back to her early childhood when she fell in love with Unsolved Mysteries and America's Most Wanted. When Stacy was five, she got mad at a babysitter who wouldn't let her watch the evening news. These days, she spends her free time listening to true crime podcasts or watching documentaries on the subject.

She has been telling stories for as long as she can remember, and as child would often get into trouble for trying to convince friends her wild tales were true. Now she puts her creativity to better use by writing page-turning stories that leave readers begging for more.

Nolon King writes fast-paced psychological thrillers set in the glitzy world of entertainment's power players with a bold, insightful voice. He's not afraid to explore the darker side of human nature through stories featuring families torn apart by secrets and lies.

Nolon loves to write about big questions and moral

quandaries. How far would you go to cover up an honest mistake? Would you destroy your career to protect your family? How much of your soul would you sell to get the life of your dreams? Would you cheat on your husband to keep your children safe? Would you give in to a stalker's demands to save your marriage?

Also By Nolon King and Stacy Claflin

Dead For Good

Dead For Good

Left For Dead

Dead Of Night

Wake The Dead

Dead For Life

Once Upon A Crime

Once Upon A Crime

Twice Upon A Lie

Three Times a Murder

Stand Alone Novels

Lost and Found

A Simple Kill

Blown

Miserable Lies

Secrets We Keep

Close To Home

Heat To Obsession

Tell Me No Lies

Fade To Black